The Elephant in the Ivy

THE ELEPHANT IN THE IVY

A whimsical and irreverent spy novel–of sorts–in the beautiful and mysterious New England college underground.

ALEXANDER GREENGAARD

Pima Open Digital Press, Open TXT- Tucson Arizona

Cover art and design by Caitlin B Alexander

CONTENTS

INTRODUCTION

I really did look around a lot before I decided to write this. The goal was to find something to share with adults who wanted to get into the habit of reading but found literature intimidating. There's actually plenty of that, and I certainly don't do it better than the sorts of people who go and write a book in Amsterdam for a year. The other thing I needed was something free and open, so that everyone could have access. And there's the rub, right there. The free stuff was either too old or I didn't like it. And the stuff I liked wasn't free.

So I either had to complain about it or I had to write it. I decided to complain about it. This lasted a while, and then I got tired of that, and decided to write it.

This book is a little bit for classrooms. I want it to be a companion to lessons about literature. I want teachers to be able to assign it to the whole class without having to worry about the budget or how to get a hold of copies. I want adult learners working on their high school equivalency diplomas to have something that helps them practice that doesn't feel daunting or stuffy. I want teachers to reuse and remix this so that you can have it for your own classroom purposes– just make sure to include a note that I was the original author.

This book is also for my friends, students, and family. If you know me personally, you're the audience I'm writing this for. I hope it makes you laugh. I hope it makes you want to keep reading. If you know anyone who says "I want to get back into reading," I hope you'll tell them that your friend wrote a book and it's light and easy to read and you should try it because it's free anyway.

A COMPANION TO OPEN ELA

This book is also a companion novel to Open ELA: A Complete Course in Reading and Language Arts. I've linked the first eight chapters of this book to the Understanding Literature unit of that one. I've also created a Classroom Edition that connects to concepts in Open ELA, hopefully helping students to understand major concepts in modern fiction. Or, you can just read the book, no harm no foul.

Oh, and if you're looking at a print version and would rather have this book for free, head on over to elephantbook.net and get the free one. I won't tell anyone.

DEDICATION

For Nika and Grace.

THE ELEPHANT IN THE IVY

ONE

"My aim is true."

Alison Ashe spoke the words through an anxious knot as she scanned Olive Street for the third time, expecting some detail to miraculously change. Three Gamma sisters were en route to Emery House. To the west, a pair of young lovers were passing through the gardens on a romantic evening. Her heart was pounding and she was curiously out of breath– tough medicine for a quiet September stroll through the Quad. The mantra helped, to the extent that it could, to steel her nerves. But a shudder still powered through the nape of her neck and shook her shoulders visibly. Surely an onlooker wouldn't give her a second thought. Unless that onlooker was *in play.* Should that reality arise, a few words on the cover of an Elvis Costello record wouldn't be of much use.

The crest of Anthony Keane's baseball cap was just visible above the ivy-laden balcony wall of the upper deck of Churchill House, where he kept watch. Alison reached for her handset to ask for another all-clear, but Tony had beaten her to the punch.

"It's time, Aly," blared Tony, a little too loudly in her earpiece. "The asset is in a brown duffel coat. Finish the drop and proceed to Frank Hall."

"The play's the thing," replied Alison, breathing through another shudder and starting the ascent.

"Good luck," Tony said, more softly, when he saw her take foot.

"You mean break a leg," Alison countered. "Don't wanna jinx it."

"Right. Break a leg," he remembered.

"And you call yourself one of the Lord Chamberlain's Men."

The brown duffel coat rounded the corner of Thayer and Euclid with enough clearance for Alison to hook a sharp left after the drop and move in on Frank Hall, the Life Sciences Lab. He had shoulder-length black hair and a day's worth of rough stubble. He also had a stack of yellow flyers in his left hand, one of which he passed enthusiastically to one of the Gammas. When another sorority sister from the pack idly reached out for one, he looked flustered for a moment and handed her a flyer from the bottom of the stack.

Good, she thought. *At least I'm not the only asset still struggling with tradecraft.*

Alison made sure he could see her silver college pin secured firmly to the right lapel of her topcoat as she moved closer. With bright eyes, he offered her the flyer at the top of the stack.

"Did you hear The Format is doing a reunion tour? They're playing the Strand next Saturday."

Alison studied the flyer for something out-of-place. She didn't have a lot of time, and she wanted to avoid looking conspicuous. She tried to memorize the sheet as she folded a crease down its center and slipped it in the front pocket of her backpack.

First off, 14/19/20 is not a date, so that's something.

She kicked a few ideas around in her mind's eye as she ascended the steps to the lab. Casually, she extended a hand toward one of the large handles on the double-doors. *Locked. So much for casual.* She gave the other side a try as well, fully aware it would not open, but the heart wants what the heart wants. To the right of the doors she noticed a keycard reader. "Yup," she blurted out in a self-deprecating huff. "It's like I've never seen a door before." Through the glass, she could see a graduate student descending a spiral staircase, assuredly on his way out. He had a clean, dirty-blonde crew cut and a look in his eye that indicated he would most definitely cure cancer this week; next week, tops.

Okay, Aly, she thought. *Let's lean into that tragic energy that comes so naturally to you. The boy looks like he could use a damsel to save.*

She unzipped her backpack and started digging around, trying to look frustrated as she searched frantically for a keycard that wasn't there. She pulled out a five-subject notebook and tucked it under her arm, stashed a Sharpie between her teeth, and started furiously shaking out an Economics textbook. Mr. Wonderful was almost to the door when she dropped the book, lost her balance from the change in equilibrium, and biffed it on the concrete.

She was fine. The Lord Chamberlain's Men had the best single-combat training of all the assets in play. If she wanted to give the boy the ol' Ha-Du-Ken and make off with his keycard while he twitched on the steps, she could. But damsels had more leverage than street fighters, and she felt plenty empowered from where she was. On the concrete. Empowered and crumpled.

"Oh my god!" cried Malibu Biology Ken as he burst through the stage-left double door. "Are you okay?"

"I'm alright," she let out in a tortured whimper. "I was just–" she trailed off there. He could fill in the blanks with his all-beef chivalry.

I was just leveraging your hospitality to break into your laboratory and steal priceless intelligence. Who's a good boy? Are you a good boy?

At this point, Alison wasn't sure even the truth would deter him. His "Mission Accomplished" banner was flying high as he helped her up and held the door, motioning her through with a sweeping gesture.

He is a good boy.

She made haste to a private alcove near the stairwell and reproduced the flyer for further examination. Her breathing still hadn't returned to normal and she was vaguely worried she might have inadvertently common-law married Sir Lancelot back there. When she caught herself chewing on a strand of too-straight medium-brown hair, she knew she wasn't focusing.

"Hey, Tony. Do you think you could take a crack at this flyer? I can take a picture of it and send it to your phone."

"Better not," Tony countered. "It's not a secure line. Elephants can compromise a civilian iPhone. Stay on the com and you can describe it to me."

"Too late," Alison replied through a smirk.

"Well, in that case I'd be happy to. Are you in the lab?"

"If the lobby counts." Alison started taking in the floor plan, charting the least conspicuous route to the third floor and considering exit strategies in the unlikely event of a water landing, or more plausibly, a greased-piggy style chase sequence. "Oink, oink, nerds!"

"What?"

"Nothing."

"Okay, Aly. Is there any sort of locker area?" Tony had grown to accept Alison's frequent and perplexing non sequiturs over the coms.

"I'll have a look."

Alison took a few strides up the stairs with all the confidence and wherewithal of a prairie dog walking into a cobra prom. *I have got to calm down.* She switched her earpiece from the com to her phone and thumbed through her recently played tracks, landing on Accidents Will Happen by Elvis Costello and the Attractions. *Oh, Elvis.* The music sent a shockwave of resolution through her body, straightening her posture and imbuing her with self-assurance. It was like she had a Fonzi* switch.

*A note to younger readers: Fonzi, AKA Arthur Fonzerelli, AKA The Fonz, was a character on an old-timey TV show called Happy Days. He was very cool and he wore a leather jacket and he could make a broken jukebox work again by hitting it. And he had a motorcycle.

At the top of the stairs, the hallway branched off in three directions. The south wing revealed a few nondescript classrooms and offices. Nothing of interest. Just east of the fork, an alcove tapered into two doors labeled Lab Eqp and Custodial. The north wing was blocked off by thick, clear strips of plastic. It looked ominous, like an antechamber in a slaughterhouse or Stephen King's breakfast nook. As she inched closer to it, a knot of nervous energy was born in her stomach and bubbled up to her throat, where it came out as a giggle because Elvis Costello had just come in with the chorus and it was too much.

A wave of tense curiosity slowed her to a crawl as she pushed a sheet of thick translucent membrane to the side and peeked into what lay beyond. She was moving like molasses. Dream running. Her skin turned electric as cold air rushed out of the space she had opened in the barrier. It swirled around her, a blood transfusion of adrenaline and existential dread.

"Excuse me."

Her soul jumped out of her body, passing a crescendo of crackling fireworks in her skull on the way out. She turned slowly, pounding at her inner jukebox for any remaining essence of Fonzi. A woman manifested, John Lennon glasses, her hair in a tight brown bun secured with a long golden pin. Cute for the Grim Reaper. Alison let out a sharp, indecipherable syllable and prepared for a sloppy, unflattering last breath.

"Excuse me," the woman repeated. "You need your lab coat if you're going into the North Lab. Do you keep it in your locker?" She gestured toward the door with the Lab Eqp placard.

"Oh, right. Duh," Alison choked out, practicing her Pulitzer Prize acceptance speech. "Yeah. Yes. Locker. It's– in my locker." *Cool, Alison. Icy*, she thought as she Fonzi'd over to the Lab Equipment room. It was bigger than the storage closet she was expecting. Clean, neatly-labeled cabinets bearing a buffet helping of goggles, gloves, and Bunsen burners. She took in the scene as she switched back to her coms.

"Aly. Alison. Do you copy?"

Oh, boy. Tony only called her Alison if he was worried.

She must have zoned out a little. She glanced at her phone. Elvis was done crooning and The White Stripes had moved in with Blue Orchid.

"This is Alison," she copied back with a spoonful of faux-southern honey in her voice. Tony let out a relieved sigh. "Found the lockers. Any luck with The Format?"

"Good. Yeah," he replied. "Are the lockers numbered?"

"No, names. Grad students, I'm guessing. Looks like a student lab."

Tony was silent for a moment. He must have been hoping for numbers. Alison could hear furious typing in the background. "Any Nates or Sams?"

"Yeah, a Nathan Russel."

"That's it! Try 14, 19, 20."

Alison made an indignant huff. "I said that first," she whined sarcastically. She was starting on the locker. "Fourteen is not a month."

"Did you say it, or did you think it really loud?" he teased.

"How did you figure out Nathan Russel?" she changed the subject.

"Oh, just a wild guess. Wikipedia says the members of The Format were Nate Ruess and Sam Means."

"Gotcha. Good thinking," She said, idly. "That band is not getting back together by the way. Those Gamma sisters are going to be so confused when they show up at some smooth jazz concert." The locker emitted a satisfying click as its tumblers fell into place. "I'm in."

"You're such a dork, Alison. Never change."

The locker was empty albeit a single ivory figurine, four inches tall, depicting a Gupta king on an intricate throne.

"Wha–" was all Alison could muster.

"What is it?" Tony inquired. "Notes? Journals? Spreadsheets?"

"It's–" she could scarcely believe it herself. "The Raja."

Tony was silent. He must have been taking a half-rusted slide rule to the mental calculus on this one. The prime objective. Sitting in a locker on an intel drop. She scooped The Raja into her bag as she waited for Tony's take on this one. It did seem a bit odd on second inspection. The figure wasn't a king, per se. Female features. More of a Mantri than a Raja. Through the com, she could hear Tony's laptop snap shut.

"Deuce," he exhaled. "This was an ambush. I'm seeing company."

"Deuce," she mirrored, adding a couple more for good measure. "Double deuce. Did they ping your phone? Elephants."

Tony's voice was being swallowed up by a cacophony of grunts, pants, and bangs. "Don't worry about the phone."

"Tony. This is my fault," Alison forcefully whispered into the com.

"Don't worry about the phone, Alison. Just get out of there!" The com went dead there. Dead people don't talk.

Alison took a deep, shuddering breath and switched her earpiece back to her phone. "Speak of the devil," she exclaimed as she hammered through the door and shot down the south wing. Nate Ruess's melancholy tenor was thundering over the orchestra in the final chorus of Be Calm. Alison's stomach churned out a one-syllable laugh and she hit a full sprint down the hallway.

Her flat-footed gait and threadbare gray Converse All-Stars produced pounding echoes in the narrow corridor. That, or another set of footfalls. She didn't dare look.

Around the next corner she could see the dim red glow of what she urgently hoped was an emergency exit sign.

Alison's All-Stars squealed against the laminate flooring as she rounded the corner, nearly sending her through the opposite wall. She lept for the emergency exit. The heavy metal door cracked against its jamb like a thunderclap, resonating past her down the hallway. It was locked.

"That's against the fire code," she blurted in frustration. A lot was happening. It was the only thing she could think to say. Now that she wasn't moving, she confirmed that the second set of footsteps was definitely not hers. She crouched down out of sight behind the sharp corner landing and waited for the sound to get louder.

"My aim is true."

A leg came into her field of view and she tumbled low, taking her pursuant down like a linebacker. A tangle of arms and legs crashed into the far wall as Alison somersaulted over the toppling body. She caught a glimpse of his face as his shoulders battered squarely into the blue and white tiles. It was Malibu Ken. The exit light flashed against a polished silver pin on his lapel.

It was Malibu Ken– and– he was an Elephant.

For a split second, his eyes looked unable to focus as he reoriented himself. Alison wasn't going to give him time to fight. His head was practically in her lap. Her training and instinct took over. She was in full Costello-mode. She threaded her arm under his chin and reached for the nape of his neck, right at the fold of the collar. She closed her eyes and twisted. And that was it.

At the end, his features fell into a look of indignance

and irritation. But he didn't say anything. Dead people don't talk.

Alison Ashe walked home with a heavy feeling in her chest. She had walked right into an ambush. Two asset identities were compromised. She had killed a man. And Tony was dead. Tony was dead, and it was her fault. She looked down at her palm, in which she carried a gleaming silver pin, the likeness of an elephant etched into its surface. Another lump manifested in her stomach. This time, it stayed there.

***

"Hey."
"Hey Aly."
"Sorry I got you killed."
"It's okay."

TWO

"The game is called Chaturanga," Alison said across a two-top table over the rustling din of the lunch crowd. Paige Hall offered only a blank stare. Alison gave her a minute. She wanted this conversation to be shrouded in mystery, bubbling with dramatic flair– as it was when Tony first explained it to her. She steepled the tips of her fingers together, both elbows secured on the table, and nodded slightly.

"Chaturanga," Paige repeated.

"It's named after an ancient Indian board game: an early predecessor to chess." Paige was silent. Her mouth tightened and her brow furrowed a bit as a short strand of auburn hair fell out of her pixie cut and into her face. Alison continued. "It means 'four factions.'"

"I thought it meant 'four feet,'" Paige interrupted.

Alison was impressed, a smirk curling on her lip. She changed posture as if to ask "How do you know that?"

Paige answered the unspoken question, or perhaps the awkward silence. "It's a yoga pose."

Alison wasn't sure how to process that knowledge. It somehow made the whole thing seem silly for the moment. Perhaps it was a bit silly. In any case, the game was very serious and important to her, and from what she could tell, anyone else in play. She continued.

"The original rules of Chaturanga are mostly lost to history. We know it was played on an eight by eight board and that the game revolved around the movements of four divisions of units: footmen, cavalry, chariots, and elephants." Alison paused a moment to take a sip of her tea. It sputtered through the straw, chipping away slightly at the moody ambiance she was attempting to evoke. "Each unit had a unique move-set. Its own way to gain position against an opponent. There's also a Raja, a king, which we assume was to be defended, and a Mantri, his counselor."

"Like the queen," Paige's eyes were more engaged now. She was intrigued. "So, what's the deal at Bauer? What's the game?"

"Pizza Margherita and two plates," Paige jumped as the waiter dropped the meal on its rack in the center of the table, steam swirling in elegant patterns between them. "Anything else I can get for you?"

Alison gave a little smile. "This looks great, thanks."

The two made an unspoken agreement not to touch the pizza until it or the conversation had cooled sufficiently. Alison took the interruption as an opportunity to briefly study Paige. She was compact in stature and spoke with a bubbly spark. An All-American gymnast in high school. She was quick-witted and thoughtful. Alison could picture her dropping from an air-duct on an unsuspecting Elephant asset, a look of dread and confusion on his agape, privilege-chiseled jaw. Paige went for a sort-of grungy look these days. Acid-washed 501s. Tattered brown canvas bomber, a mauve hoodie peeking out from beneath. Piercings. Alison had never considered herself posh before, but next to Paige she felt posh. And tall. She was losing focus. She clapped her hands and started in on Paige's question.

"Chaturanga is a game of position and capture played between four factions, in this case representing specific college departments, over the course of the academic year at Bauer. Each faction may recruit nine assets, essentially field agents, to engage in tactical espionage missions to improve their positions toward the prime objectives."

"The prime-"

"Each faction defends a small, ivory statuette of a Raja: actual artifacts from the Gupta Empire," Alison was on a roll. She felt like Ewen McGregor's Obi Wan explaining the ways of the Jedi to young Anakin, which is to say slightly hokey, but leaning into it. "A Raja must be displayed in plain sight in a faction's territory. If captured and held until the end of the second term, it's worth nine points."

"So it's Capture the Flag," Paige intuited in a low, lengthy tone, her brain engaged in a light mental-gymnastic tumbling pass.

"Essentially, yeah," she shrugged. "But with a few important differences. I think of Capture the Flag as a game about running. Chaturanga is more about planning, talking, thinking one step ahead of your opponent. It's slower, more methodical. Missions can take weeks to develop. Position is gained and lost. Alliances are made and broken."

"Do you wear little football flags around all year?" Paige posited through a giggle.

"We do," Alison said, leaning out of an ambient shadow

and gesturing to her coat. "Assets wear college pins on their right lapel. The pin is affixed to its base with a magnet. Pull the magnet off an asset and she's dead. Your faction receives one point for eliminating an opposing asset."

"Out of the game? For the rest of the year?"

"That's right. And they can no longer talk about the game. No sharing intelligence, no plotting, no planning, no warning teammates of impending danger. Dead people don't talk."

Alison produced a second pin from her pocket and slid it under the pizza rack toward Paige, who started idly examining it. On its front face, a beautiful relief of the Bauer College seal. Paige pulled on the seal, releasing it from its base. It was heartier than she'd imagined, requiring a forceful tug. The hidden side had an etching, equally beautiful, of an infantry soldier at attention.

Alison went on. "The underside depicts your faction's symbol. Ours is the Footman. They actually change each year depending on how your team ranks."

"So is that last place?"

"Sure is. The Lord Chamberlain's Men, AKA the Theatre Department, is very much the underdog these days."

Paige was ready for pizza. She pulled three slices to her plate and started voraciously demolishing the nearest one. Alison was glad to have a friend who could eat and didn't have any baggage about it. A fair share of her high school crew would give her judgy looks over their kale salads when Alison so much as thought about a carb. She smiled as she grabbed a slice and continued talking through mouthfuls of Buffalo mozzarella.

"Engineering won last year, so they received the coveted rank of Elephant. Psychology earned the rank of Chariot, the English department came in third to become the Cavalry, and that leaves us, the humble Footmen."

Paige looked contemplative as she noshed away at a second slice. She abruptly pulled the top off her Dr. Pepper and wolfed down a massive gulp, leaving a trace of the black cherry elixir at the edge of her mouth. She toweled down with an errant sleeve and looked Alison in the eye. "Why?" she asked, finally. "Why do you do this?"

"I mean, there is a *technical* answer to that question," Alison started. She tried for another swig of tea but was denied by the cruel sputter of straw against empty vessel. Paige tore the top off Alison's cup and decanted a helping of Dr. Pepper from her own. Alison nodded in appreciation and continued. "There is an undergraduate prize awarded each year: The Thomas Carpenter Prize for Elocution. College departments vote on the winner. But there's no actual contest, and the whole thing seemed arbitrary to the various academic leads. So, years ago, four department heads proposed a chess tournament to determine the winner of their collective votes. And, over time, the ante kept getting upped until we have what we have today: Chaturanga, the secret abomination."

Paige threw an eyebrow. "But there are like 40 departments now."

"Yeah. Stacking four votes is now functionally a hollow gesture. I don't think it ever really mattered, actually. I interpret it as a sort of grand protest to the pomp and circumstance that academia is always putting on completely meaningless things."

Paige smiled. It was a bright, mischievous, smile. She

was getting it. "So, it's a big, inconsequential, secret underground club that does cloak-and-dagger spy missions, but just for fun?"

Alison put a finger to her lip and considered how silly it all sounded in Paige's concise summary.

"Yes."

***

Alison took a beat to absorb the lush, gothic beauty of the campus as she and Paige veered off George Street past the steps of Connecticut Hall and onto the main mall. Fall foliage lit the oaks and maples aflame, a few crimson stars spiraling down toward the base of the massive Ionic columns that guarded the egress to John A. Bauer Library. The columns sent the eye upward, toward the heavens, where the structure was embellished by a dramatic Hellenistic frieze, complete with Zeus's eagles to protect the coveted knowledge within.

The sheer heft of the concourse reminded Alison of how fortunate she felt to be studying at Bauer, and by extension, her deeply rooted passion for theatre. Anchored by an early love of language and literature, accented regularly by the whirlwind of nervous commotion pervasive to her mind and body in performance, theatre charged her every particle with love and joy and fear and epinephrine. Theatre demanded that she take in the language, to embody it and become it: to channel its eldritch energy through the conduit of her body and release it in a rogue wave. She breathed in sharply. *I am so stupid lucky*, she thought.

Alison was on full scholarship. She balanced a full

course load with work as a carpenter in the scene shop, and occasional moonlighting as a bartender at a hipster spot downtown called The Eddy. Even then, she had to take out student loans to keep up. Contrary to popular belief, there are poor neighborhoods in New Haven. Aly grew up sharing a one-bedroom apartment with her mom in Smith Hill. She got the room– her mother would sleep on a pull-out in the living room. Sometimes she told herself that a BFA in theatre was a bit of a fool's gambit if she had any notion of changing her stars. But then, looking out at the neatly-trimmed mall, its crisp, baleful New England architecture in full bloom, she was tidily reminded that "I went to Bauer" was something of a skeleton key to many of life's sternly-guarded gates.

The autumn-touched deciduous trees lining the mall looked like torches adorning an ancient corridor. She looked over at Paige. Her legs were ridiculously short compared to Alison's somewhat lanky frame, and she took nearly twice as many steps to move at the same pace. She had her hands in her pockets, which she occasionally removed to crack a few contemplative knuckles.

"I have some questions," Paige blurted, breaking several-minutes' silence. Alison nodded her forward. "First, why are you recruiting so late? The game's been going since August."

Alison smiled. "The Lord Chamberlain's Men are often targeted early in the game. Theatre majors are seen by the other divisions as weak-willed, lacking in mental faculty. We're trying something new this year: running a short roster."

"How does that work?" Paige inquired, gears spinning behind her light brown eyes.

"The first few months typically involve gathering intelligence on opposing factions. Figuring out their rosters, whereabouts, movements. We figure running a short list will keep them guessing, maybe drive them crazy trying to unveil the identities of operatives that don't exist."

Paige gave an approving chuckle. "How many are you running?"

"Six. We want to keep it there. So, in the unfortunate but inevitable event of an asset's demise, we have the elbow room to swap out for a fresh soul. Believe it or not, dear Paige, I was the first of the Lord Chamberlain's Men to draw blood. So I've been given the honor to select my new partner. I should also mention at this point that I very much got my last partner killed. I'm a wild card, Paige!"

Paige let out a hearty laugh at that. Alison's energy was infectious. But after a moment's respite, her face fell in hesitation. "Okay, that brings me to my next question: why me?"

Alison was startled to think that Paige had even an inkling of self-doubt. To her, Paige was an obvious choice. Sharp, ambitious, athletic. She was completely trustworthy and good company to boot. Though they didn't have much social contact outside of school, Paige and Alison bonded last spring semester during a production of King Lear. They played sisters Reagan and Goneril, whose vile aspirations drove them to gouge out the eyes of the lecherous Lord Gloucester. They had spent many loopy, twilight hours together in Lyman Hall, memorizing lines and working intricate blocking. They had also taken Stage Combat Two together, required for the roles, and found trust in each other as sparring partners. Her somersault-takedown of Malibu Ken had, in fact, been pulled right out of Paige's playbook.

While there is no bond greater than the one shared by two undergrads gouging a man's eyes out with four-inch heels, that wasn't Alison's angle on this pass. "The game," she began, "has become a bit of a boy's club. There's too many, they're too smug, and they're incredibly patronizing: even the ones on your own team!"

"So you just want another girl," Paige offered.

Alison could see traces of skepticism start to creep into Paige's expression. "Just another girl isn't going to cut it. It's gotta be you, pumpkin. You're fast. You can fight. You think for yourself. And I trust you."

Paige scrunched her face. "I don't know, Aly. It's just–kind of weird."

"Paige, listen." Alison stopped walking and squared her shoulders to face Paige directly. The sun was starting to fall beneath the Doric colonnade that ran across the ingress of Manning Hall. A streetlamp flicked on overhead, illuminating Alison in warm amber light. She paused to gather her thoughts, perforated by a sharp gulp. "Everything I've ever fought for, I had to fight harder. Privilege, disadvantage– they're irrevocably woven into society, and I get it. I can accept that. I can work with that. And it's fine. Well, it's not fine, but it's the canvas we're dealing with."

Alison crossed her arms and looked south as the last of the sunlight faded rapidly on the lush, trim grass beyond. She exhaled deeply and looked back at Paige. She went on. "This game is the first thing I've experienced with any semblance of an even playing field. As much as they talk down and condescend, they don't cheat. So, if I'm at my best, I can, for the first time in my life, face the world with a pinch of objectivity. Without wondering about the role of my circumstances on my outcomes. And you know what, Paige? I think you and I could be the real deal. Being underestimated– it might actually put us at an advantage. We could change the whole picture!"

The sun was gone, now. A few more streetlamps snapped to life, breathing soft light onto the long walkway between Hope College and Arnold Lab, parallel to the sweeping red brick architecture of Waterman Street. A long shadow came into focus across their path as a light popped into existence to the west.

"Okay," said Paige. "Let's– let's beat up some boys."

"That's the spirit," Alison cried with a wave of ribaldry. "Good timing, too."

Paige looked up as Alison bestowed a silver pin onto her lapel. She followed Alison's eyes westward.

"Because that guy's been following us for twelve blocks."

THREE

Alison and Paige shared a cheery hug and parted ways there at the north steps of Faunce House, where Waterman street bisected the spruce mall, illuminated by the Victorian lamps that lined the thoroughfare. Paige went west, toward Hope College, hands in her pockets, a little bounce in her step. A coquettish smile crept across her slight features, hidden under the dim lights.

Alison crossed Waterman and headed east, toward Walter and Norwood, wondering who her long-legged shadow would follow. She dared not look. She produced her phone, affixing her earbuds as she hung a left toward the Urban Environmental Lab. She flicked through her playlist until she found the familiar red cover of OMNI by Minus the Bear. Bright synthesizers pulsed melodic candy over driving, upbeat drums as Alison slipped the phone back into her pocket, taking a quick glance for movement in its reflection as she pressed forward. "Hm," she whispered quietly to herself, picking up the pace as Leeds Theatre appeared distantly in her field of vision. "Freckles."

She took off suddenly, hooking a hard left at the Page Robinson Building toward Angell Street. The passage was crowded with obstacles. Poplars lined the street side. Low walls, stairs and banisters, and various architectural features jutted out from the long building. The hall cut away at its corner revealing three beautifully illuminated floors. Alison popped over a railing, stumbling a little as she landed on the soft ground below. Classroom windows streaked by on her right as she avoided tamarack trees and their enormous errant seedlings. She was on an elevated platform that inclined toward a second cut-out at the far end of the hall.

Alison leapt across a massive gap that stood between the platform and the second floor of the building, light flooding through the ingress from within. She only had a couple steps of clearance before the hard edge spilled out to the steps below. Off she went, folding her legs slightly and bracing for impact. The landing took her palms all the way to the hard concrete as her legs absorbed the massive shock. *Nothing broken. Keep running.*

Alison loved the sensation of running. The heavy heartbeat, the deep, focused breathing. Her feet pounding beneath as her arms stretched out in front, grasping at the swiftly flowing air. Running was an elevated state. She could push her body to its limits, feel the acceleration, watch the world blur around her. But even more than that, running meant control. She could move as she saw fit, a gust of wind or a crashing wave, and nobody could stop her or tell her "no." Unless they could catch her.

She made a hard right past the UEL Lab. Here, the surface level tapered up to several humanities buildings. A tunnel portal cut a clear passage through to Thayer Street. When Alison rounded the corner into the tunnel she accelerated into a sprint, the chorus of My Time drowning in the resonant echo of her steps.

Red brick archways dotted with cylindrical drop lighting fixtures flew above her line of sight as she picked up the pace until she was hit with the reverberating wave of a baritone shout.

"Alison!" the voice reflected against the sonic prism. "I just want to talk!"

It took a few steps to slow her stride to an eventual stopping point. She stood there for a moment, facing the open mouth of the corridor and Thayer Street beyond. She waited for the steps to close in. When she was satisfied, she pivoted into an impatient pose, arms akimbo, and finally got her first good look at Freckles.

He wasn't as tall as she was expecting. Five ten, but absurdly lanky. Legs to Chattanooga. As promised, freckles kissed his pale cheeks. And the whole ridiculous sundae was topped off by a perfectly shaped, dusty red pompadour. It jiggled like strawberry Jell-O as he approached. He lifted his palms in surrender as his smug smile hit the light of an overhead canister. *Rats! He was cute. Losing focus, losing focus.*

"Okay," Alison offered, still out of breath. "Talk."

"Okay," he replied, his face contorting as he conjured exactly what to say. Alison glanced at the lapel of his charcoal peacoat. Silver pin. No surprises there, but it was nice to know that he was an enemy asset and not some creeper. He opened his mouth to speak, but instead of words, a barrage of cannon fire came bursting down the corridor. Or, at least, that's what it sounded like. Shots in rapid succession, flying past her and through her, bass rumbling in her chest. The reality was worse– well, worse for him at any rate. He turned his head to reveal Paige

Hall, comin' in hot, a locomotive with centipede legs. He tried to square off as she let out a feral battle cry.

Alison, taking advantage of the flank, put a well-placed roundhouse kick in the crook of his left leg. His knee buckled to the ground. Paige dropped a shoulder, allowing her forearm to smash into the stranger's midsection. His twisted frame tumbled to the ground. Alison and Paige circled to cut off his exit as he rolled over onto his back, hands still in surrender position. He let out a dilapidated cough, eyes wild and confusion plastered onto his expression.

"Okay," he repeated. It was all he could seem to emit.

Alison shifted her posture as her mind settled. She looked completely in control of the situation by the time she broke the silence.

"It appears that some introductions are in order," she said at last. "Everyone here knows who I am, apparently." She gestured an open hand to Strawberry Pompadour before folding her arms. He sat up. When he placed his hands on the concrete to stand, Paige shook her head, and he stayed put.

"Reed Baker," he said, a measure of calm returning to his voice. "I'm Cavalry."

"Let's see some ID, Reed Baker," Paige interjected, looking excitable by Alison's account. Reed produced his wallet and tossed it to Paige. She opened it, turned it over, and dumped its contents onto Reed's lap. A student ID tumbled away from him. Paige picked it up, tossing his empty wallet into his chest with the same motion. She examined the ID, then looked back at him, overblown skepticism in her expression.

Alison chimed in here. "Hi, Reed Baker. This is–"

"Maverick," Paige cut her off, a dramatic flair in her voice. Reed smiled.

"We don't really do codenames, dear," Alison hit back.

"Yet," Paige replied, finger guns extended. She continued "Alright, then, Reed Baker. You may call me Paige Hall."

"Pleased to meet you, Paige Hall. And pleased to finally meet you in person, Alison Ashe."

"Okay, Cavalry," Paige continued, a wild spark in her voice, "Let's get down to brass tacks. What's your business with the Lord Chamberlain's Men? Are you gonna sing or are we gonna have to put this canary in the coal mine? Give him something to sing about. Black lung! You can sing about that. In the coal mine." If she was excitable before, now she was an animal. Alison had never seen this side of her, and was loving every second. Reed looked over at Alison for guidance.

Alison shrugged, unable to contain a smile at Paige's intense bad cop initiative. "You– can answer the first question."

Reed exhaled. "Okay. Well, to start, Cavalry's having a rough go this year. The Elephants are all over us. We've lost three assets already, and we're pretty sure the other six are compromised. We've ID'd maybe four assets, total. No Elephants."

"Sucks for you!" chimed Paige.

Alison cleared her throat. "I mean– she's kind of right, bud. Your fumble only benefits us."

"And now you've handed us your own skinny jeans-wearin' heinie on a silver plate as a bonus!"

"Perhaps, Paige," Alison added, her cool demeanor in

sharp contrast to Paige's unbridled passion. "Let's hear what the nice man has to say."

Reed continued. "Yes, I see the merits of popping my token here and now–"

"Like the head off a squirrel," Paige threw in. She was pacing now.

"Graphic," Reed went on, "Yes, you could very much just kill me now. But, I have another proposition that I hope you'll consider. The Elephants have an early lead. They are last year's winners by a good margin. Also by a good margin, Footmen and Cavalry lost last year. Now, I don't know how far along you are, but I don't see much of a shot at the Cavalry winning this year. However, I think it's very possible that we have a shared interest."

He stopped for a moment, perhaps to offer Paige another opportunity for ridicule and/or physical violence. She simply shifted her weight and rested her hands on her hips.

"Our factions don't have to win to gain position. We just have to make sure the Elephants lose."

Alison perked up a bit at this. "I'm listening," she encouraged.

"The first thing I'd propose is a month's ceasefire between Cavalry and Footmen. We want to shift some of the balance in your favor, but we need to trust that it won't wipe us out completely."

Paige jumped in here. "Looks to me like we've established no trust whatsoever at this point."

"That is something I hope to remedy," Reed replied, reaching into his coat's inner pocket and retrieving an ivory statuette. He stretched forward and placed it on the ground as far from his person as he could reach. Alison walked over and picked it up, examining it under the yellow tunnel light. It was real.

"Reed Baker," she said, rotating the Raja between her fingers as she spoke, "Are you, perchance, a sweet little moron?"

"I am fully aware that this move could be costly. It doesn't matter. Like I said, Cavalry's game isn't to win, necessarily, but for Elephant to lose." Alison transferred the figurine to Paige as their paths crossed. Reed continued. "So, yes, you could walk away with ten points tonight instead of nine, and three enemies. Or, you could help us take Elephant off the board entirely. Those arrogant dweebs are past due for a year as Footmen."

"We certainly share that sentiment in common," said Alison. "How do you see it actually going down?"

"You walk home with the Cavalry Raja, put it on display with your own. The Elephants won't be able to resist a two-for-one. They'll start planning a heist immediately. But, it's impossible to know when. So you start controlling the flow of information."

"Hm," Alison's wheels were spinning now. "We could leak a false job. Give them an exact date and time that we'll be out of the house–"

"And we can be there to seal the trap."

Paige smiled. "A two-faction ambush."

Alison crouched to bring her face to Reed's level. Paige must have passed the idol back to her at some point, as she was holding it between her thumb and forefinger. "I like it, Reed Baker. Really, I do. And I must say, this is a doozie of an olive branch. But we need a minute to consider all the angles before we can give you the thumbs-up."

"I understand," Reed said soberly. "How about this?

Tonight, we trade the Cavalry Raja for my continued status of 'currently alive.' In a week, you will find me on the stone bench in the Garden Maze at Pembroke, noon, to work out a few details. If anything seems out of place in the meantime, you can kill me then and there."

"You drive a hard bargain, Reed Baker," said Alison, extending her hand to shake.

"Do I?"

"No. Not at all."

***

Two Cheesy Gordita Crunches later, Alison and Paige were examining the ivory figurine from a second-story bedroom in a powder blue house on West Court Street. Alison shared the house with four other juniors, two of which she knew from the Theatre program. She had grown severely tired of the dorms sophomore year, and this solution, though not very private, was more economical. Housemates Cara and Bethany were currently downstairs shouting instructions at a horror movie, and she could hear Amy crying intensely into her phone on the other side of the paper-thin wall.

Like dear Amy, Alison had nothing to hide. Except perhaps the fact that she participated in a massive, cross-campus spy game that necessitated a host of offenses that would revoke her scholarship, including but not limited to: breaking and entering, wiretapping, and assault. She had, in fact, assaulted a young man earlier this evening and it was awesome. Other than that, though, nothing to hide. Chaturanga offered opportunities to hide in plain sight. She was pretty sure she could explain the entire thing to Cara and Bethany and their only reaction would be "You're so creative, Aly."

Paige, however, totally got it. Not only that, but she was a natural. The sight of her tearing down that tunnel, hellfire in her eyes, crashing into that Cavalry. A bullet through the barrel. *Did she call herself 'Maverick?'* Alison thought. *Lucky for all of us that this little atrocity is on our own team.*

Paige looked up from the statuette, her eyes refocusing on Alison's. "So, we're gonna screw over the Cavalry, too. Right?"

Alison smiled. "Oh, pumpkin," she replied. "Of course we are."

FOUR

Sunday felt like a rude purgatory to Alison. She was brimming with nervous energy from the events of the night before. Now that the Cavalry Raja was secure, her faction had until the end of the day on Monday to display it clearly in Footman territory. The Theatre Department had plenty of excellent places to stash the goods. Their own objective was currently on display in the Great Hall at Leeds Theatre, in the thoughtfully outstretched hand of a sculpture of Hamlet, where Yorick's skull should be. The sculpture was white marble, borrowed from Mount Holyoke. The ivory of the statuette blended perfectly, though it was thematically unusual. No one seemed to mind. Now, what an all-women's college was doing with a Hamlet sculpture, Alison could not say. That play doesn't have a lot of empowered female characters, unless you count Ophelia's departure from the breathing club as a final act to keep Hamlet's crazypants mitts off her.

Four cameras, scattered throughout the hall, had vantage on the Lord Chamberlain's Raja. A fifth installation, hidden in a camera casing, emitted an infrared beam directly at the Gupta King in question. In the event of an interruption to said beam, a silent alarm was outfitted to send an APB to Control and all live assets.

The figure itself was furnished with a GPS receiver, which assets could monitor on their phones. This was all quite reassuring, or it would be, if not for the unfortunate position of facing engineers in a rival faction. They always seemed a year ahead in tech.

By Alison's math, this was fine. Each faction had unique advantages. English majors had a natural talent for cryptography and document forgery. Also, they seemed pretty up-to-date on tradecraft. Maybe they had a shared set of Le Carre's spy novels, or spent late nights memorizing The Scarlet Pimpernel. Psychology undergrads seemed to focus on tracking patterns in the movements and behaviors of the other factions. They drew up complex sorties, attempting to predict how others would react under various circumstances. And the Lord Chamberlain's Men were of course the best liars. The undergraduate career of the theatre major was finely tailored toward a life of professional deception and impersonation.

Alison was laying ponderously on a pile of clean but unfolded laundry when her phone rang. "Hey, Paige," she beamed, thankful for a fresh excuse to procrastinate on this week's homework.

"Hey, Aly. When do we deliver the thing to the place?"

"This isn't a secure line, dear heart," Alison encouraged. "We can chat about all the things and places during Critical Theory."

"Speaking of which, do you have a thesis for the Hamlet paper?"

"I have thoughts on Hamlet. Nothing revolutionary, but I think it's enough for a term paper."

Paige exhaled a frustrated little breath. "I'm stuck. Will

you pitch me your idea? Maybe it'll kick loose some dirt in the decrepit little mausoleum in my noggin?"

Alison hesitated. "Okay, well–"

"I promise I won't snag your idea," Paige reassured, "if that's what you're worried about."

"No, no. It's not that." Alison bit her lip. Paige, of course, had no way of detecting this, but knew instinctively that this was a lip-biting pause. "It's just– easy to dismiss and I'm worried that people will think it's dumb."

"I'm sure it's not dumb."

"You haven't heard it yet."

"Okay, Alison," Paige said through a sigh. "Please tell me your dumb idea and break the earwax rocks in my head."

"Okay. I think Hamlet is funny."

"Like, the character?"

"No, the whole play. I think it's a comedy."

Paige chewed on this. "Isn't it, like, our cultural milestone for dark and broody?"

"Yeah," Alison rang back, a little excitement rising in her voice as she gathered her thoughts. "I think that's our culture coloring the work so we can keep casting mopey-faced goth boys in the role. The play itself is funny. Played for laughs, I think it would get laughs."

"Everybody dies."

"That's funny, Paige!" Whether or not that was true, Alison's delivery elicited a short, sharp laugh from Paige, capped with a decisive snort. It was the first snort of many that Alison would draw out of Paige in a long friendship.

"Alison, give me a specific example of something funny in Hamlet."

"Okay, so when dude finally musters the courage to kill his stepdad, he sees a rustling behind a curtain, and instead of looking he just stabs it. He just up and stabs whoever is behind the curtain, hoping it'll be his stepdad. But it's not, it's his girlfriend's actual father! It's like some kind of twisted mistaken-identity love triangle, but with stabbing. It's Twelfth Night, but with blood fountains instead of false mustaches."

"Give me another. I'm processing."

"Next scene," Alison resounded through a chuckle, "Hamlet has just moved the body upstairs. King Claudius, evil uncle extraordinaire, walks in and says 'Where's Polonius?' Hamlet says 'At supper.'"

"At supper?"

"Yeah, Claudius is confused as well. Hamlet needs to clarify. 'Not where he eats but where he is eaten.' Like, it's supper for the worms and dude's the main course."

"Dang," said Paige. "That's cold. Aren't we supposed to feel bad? Because he's descending into madness or whatever?"

Alison smiled audibly. "Oh, Hamlet isn't crazy."

"Jesus, Aly, you buried the lede! How is Hamlet not crazy?"

"He's pretending. He only says the crazy stuff when people are watching. It's a smokescreen. To soften the blow of all the evil schemes he's plotting. No, he's not crazy, he's lucid. He knows he's probably going to die for all of his shenanigans. Providence in the fall of a sparrow and whatever. So he cracks jokes to make the best of a bad situation."

"Now he's cracking jokes?" Paige was getting incredulous.

"Constantly. And in the least opportune moments. He

jokes at Ophelia's funeral. He jokes during the duel that kills him."

Paige was running the numbers on this. "And you said it's to make the best of a bad hand?"

Alison was still working this part out. "I think so. Something like that, anyway. Some kind of grand metaphor or implicit theme. We're all gonna die anyway, so let's at least get a few good belly laughs in there before the devil takes us."

"Hm," said Paige after a few quick calculations. "Well, I'm not sure it's Hamlet, but it's definitely you. Peters is gonna hate it at any rate, if that's what you're going for."

Alison considered this. "I mean– isn't that what college is for? Taking a bold stand? Making a strong case for a wild idea? I'm living the dream!"

"Maybe they should have us write papers on Hamlet after we mount a full production of it. Oh! That reminds me! Who are you auditioning for?"

Alison offered a pause the length of a short, dramatic drumroll. "Hamlet," she said plainly.

"I mean, I love it, but why?"

"I already told you," said Alison, "he has all the good jokes."

***

The Lord Chamberlain's Men met on Monday afternoons under the proscenium of Leeds Theatre. Seven burgundy armchairs were circled at center stage, illuminated by a single follow spot. Six for active assets, one for Control. Each faction was counselled by a faculty member from its corresponding department, who could offer advice on matters, but never formulated plans or gave orders. These advisers wore pins as well, and could be eliminated, albeit for zero points. Such actions were rare, but once in a long while a team saw value in cutting off their foes from this valuable wealth of knowledge. After all, dead people don't talk.

On this sunkissed September Monday, Professor Jim Peters arrived first, and occupied an embellished, quilted armchair as assets trickled in. He quietly admired what was left of the set for The Cherry Orchard between bouts of intense scribbling on a yellow legal pad. All dads write on yellow legal pads. It's one of the unspoken laws of the universe. Aly wasn't sure if Peters even was a dad, but he had dad energy, and that was enough to earn him at least an honorary legal pad. Alison and Paige made sure to arrive fashionably late. A new asset and a captured objective practically necessitated a dramatic entrance. Arm in arm, they did not fail to make the grade.

"Gentlemen, it is my privilege to introduce the inimitable Paige Hall, newest member of the Lord Chamberlain's most esteemed." Applause was replaced with open-handed slapping of the various leather arms of the circled wing chairs and numerous shouts of "Hear, hear!" Paige would come to learn the irresistible appeal of emulating the mannerisms of stuffy, Victorian-Era British aristocrats.

A series of old-timey salutations of the "Good egg!" and "Bally ho!" variety rung in riotous unison, capped by a decisive "What say you, Page Hall?" from Control.

Paige had the floor. She surveyed the scene for clues as to how she should respond. She had never been in a British Men's Club before. She hadn't really been in any club, except for gym, which was always very stern and serious in tone. She let the silence settle, and then put forth a meager "Pip, pip?"

And the crowd went wild.

"Paige Hall," Control commanded the conversation as the bedlam trickled to a low hum. "I should now introduce you to the remainder of your unit. To your immediate left, in the burnt ember anorak, is Andy McElroy. He's our resident gearhead. He'll set you up with your com and put your head on straight in regards to technological affairs. Clockwise from Sir Andy is Ed Butler. Dramaturg by day, plotter of dastardly operations in the evening hours. Teddy Dalton is our watcher. He gathers intelligence on the movements of known enemy assets. He also moonlights as operator, as poor old Tony Pierce is no longer with us. Rest with the angels, Tony. And that leaves Brian Ward, here in the Patagonia puffer. Our runner. Sometimes you just need someone who can run like the dickens."

The undergraduates shook hands and exchanged pleasantries as Control made his way around the gauntlet.

"Surely you've already met Ms. Ashe," he said fondly.

"I have," Paige replied. "What's her specialty?"

Paige looked over at Alison, who didn't actually know the answer to this. She shrugged and looked back to Control.

"Alison is our fighter. She excels at single combat."

I do? replied Alison's stunned expression.

"Never wander down a dark alley without her." A second round of chair beating confirmed the affirmation. "Now, Paige. I'd like you to consider your talents as well. What might you offer to the Lord Chamberlain's Men?"

Paige smiled. "How bout you offer me a chair and I'll think about it?"

The meeting progressed. Alison recounted the encounter with Reed Baker of the Cavalry. Paige jumped in intermittently to enthusiastically highlight a detail or crack wise. Alison showed no exception to her budding talent for burying the lede, waiting for correct placement in the narrative to produce the Raja from the interior pocket of her topcoat. The revelation elicited a thunderous collection of British colloquialisms.

As the roaring began to dim, Control cleared his throat and eyes settled on him. "Without any errant doubt, this should convert us some position, and so should be seen as a resounding victory. Paige, Alison, bally good show. Moving forward, we must return to you. Any action we take on this will depend gravely on your answer to the following inquiry. In your gut, do you trust this Baker fellow?"

Paige was at a loss. With a glance, she offered this one up to Alison, who ruminated on every angle she could rally forth. Leaking false intel certainly couldn't hurt their position. If the Cavalry drops the ball on backup, Footmen could still reliably close the trap on their own. Even a single Elephant out of play was a worthwhile conversion. Reed Baker was the hot question. *Literally. Focus, old girl.* The Cavalry had so much to gain by helping the Footmen, and far too much to lose in deceiving them. Perhaps it didn't matter. Perhaps there was a way to squeeze more of that sweet strawberry syrup out of the lovely Reed Baker. *You know, for insurance. And no other reason.*

When the silence had become borderline audacious,

Alison spoke. "I do not trust Reed Baker. But I trust that I can manage him."

Ed Butler spoke next. "Bully, then. All in favor of proceeding?" The measure passed unanimously. "Alison, I trust you can run point on this. I want Paige with you at all times during active operations. Teddy Dalton, can you play operator?"

"That sounds most agreeable, sir."

"Splendid," Ed returned. "Do keep us abreast of the details as they develop. On to the matter of placement of our newest Gupta monarch."

After some debate, it was agreed that the Prince of Denmark did indeed have two hands, and that the Rajas would be best friends. And that surely they would be lonely if not placed in close proximity to one another. New business was conducted. Old business was conducted. Measures were voted upon. Minutes were taken. Sir Andy would set up a second laser to guard the new objective. It was then agreed upon, with no objections noted, that the device was not actually a laser, and that Sir Andy would set up a second whats-it. As the meeting neared its conclusion, Control assumed the floor once more.

"Before we part, I would be remiss not to query young Paige Hall as to whether she has yet devised a specialty to contribute to the Lord Chamberlain's Men."

Paige scrunched her mouth tightly, crossing a stray leg as she shifted in her absurdly ornate chair. The expression faded to an impish smile as she perforated the silence with the assorted poppings of a fistful of knuckles. "Yes. Quite. Rather. In regards to the matter, I should acquiesce to declare a specialty in– surprises."

And the armchair thunder rang once more.

FIVE

Backpack, earbuds, Hamlet. Check, check, check. Laptop. There you are. Coms, just in case. Coat– college pin, secured in place. Notebook, notebook. Oh! The Tempest for Paige. Hello, dear. Phone, wallet, keys. Tap, tap, tap. The ol' triple tap. And, that's everything– pants!

The ritual wasn't perfect. Alison would walk out the bedroom door sans something biweekly. Pants were a new low, however. She sniffed a thrice-worn set of olive green corduroys and sidled into them using her tried and true three-hop method. Alison gave a one-syllable laugh as she threaded a warped, brown leather belt, taking two stairs at a time towards the threshold and considering the burgeoning pattern of threes in her life. *Three taps, three hops, three weeks since I did laundry.*

On today's docket: Lyman Hall, at the secret spot, to help Paige pick an audition monologue. Spoiler alert: I already picked one for her. Stagecraft and Method before lunch hour. After lunch, find a way to put off that Hamlet paper.

Court merged into Meeting Street at about the spot where college architecture started popping up among the residential structures. The campus didn't have hard boundaries. You simply walked through a beautiful, historic neighborhood until you eventually noticed yourself on a beautiful, historic campus. The first sight of campus was West House, one of the many converted residences, just before the ostentatiously baroque steeples of Pembroke Hall met the line of sight. For some reason, West House always compelled Alison to plug in her earbuds and fire up her music.

Something between the cool morning air and the fiery autumn maples told Alison that this was a day for comfort food. Which, for her, meant The Shins. She had a habit of letting her thumb hover over Port of Morrow before succumbing to Wincing the Night Away; the former being the better record, the latter being her first introduction to this gloriously upbeat, honeyed ginger bonbon of a band. Juiced up on nostalgia and fresh air, she felt no shame skipping Sleeping Lessons and hopping right into Australia. A shuddering breath landed on a wide smile as la la's peppered the opening riff. By the time the pre-chorus arpeggios upped the intensity ante, she was in full Costello Mode, a bounce in her gait and a key to the city in her pocket.

If college buildings were intended to hearken ancient majesty, Lyman Hall definitely got the memo. The base of each structure was laden in mortarless lime brick, exploding into Florentine red above. A portcullis guarded the entrance with a magnificent arch, at which the brick began to wrap elegantly around the cylindrical base of a medieval turret, complete with conical lookout at its peak. It was in the uppermost alcove of this conservatory, in a battlement fit for Rapunzel, that Paige and Alison discovered the secret spot.

"This one made me think of you," said Alison, digging a

worn copy of The Tempest from her bag and tossing it to Paige. "Flip to Act II, Scene II. Trinculo."

"Here's neither bush nor shrub, to bear off any weather at all, and another storm brewing; I hear it sing i' the wind." Paige's voice grew as she started to visualize the shipwreck and rolling tide. "Yond same black cloud, yond huge one, looks like a foul bombard that would shed his liquor." She broke off. "Weather exposition? You read weather exposition and you thought of me?"

"Keep reading, pumpkin."

"What have we here? A man or a fish? Dead or alive? A fish: he smells like a fish; a very ancient and fish-like smell." Paige became wild-eyed as she channeled the words, crouching and making strong, emphatic crosses intermittently. "Oh," she stopped, making a realization. "Oh! I have to hide under the body! Tuck myself in?"

Alison nodded. "I was thinking we could ask Phil or Parker– one of the bigger guys– to lay downstage left in a pair of tighty-whities. And you could sort of– struggle to make him into a shelter from the storm."

"Misery acquaints a man with strange bedfellows." They laughed in unison. Paige was studying the text again. "Well, I'll start with the words and work my way down. Thanks, Aly. This is a great monologue! What are you thinking of for you?"

"Thisbe."

Paige froze in thought for a short moment as she tried to place the name. She then lit up, pointing a finger of realization at her dear friend. "From the play within a play? Midsummer Night's Dream, right? The faux-Juliet?"

"The very same."

"And it's– what? A funny death scene?"

Alison had prepared this answer. "Yeah. She finds her lover Pyramus dead and can't go on living without him. But it's actually Francis Flute, the bellows mender, playing the role. So he kind of hams it up for his royal audience. I see it as a license to overact."

Paige was tentatively onboard. "Okay, yeah. That's pretty– you."

Alison was pacing at this point, gesturing heavily to areas of the stage as she described a draft of the blocking. "I was thinking I would blow up two balloons and stuff them in my shirt. And then pop them with a pin taped to a prop dagger for the big death. And farewell friends, thus Thisbe ends. Adieu. Pop! Adieu. Pop! Adieu."

Paige laughed as Alison fell to the floor in outlandish visage, but her face soon fell into something more skeptical. "You want to do an elaborate practical gag for your audition monologue? For Hamlet?"

"They need to see that Hamlet can be funny."

"I mean– don't get me wrong, it's very bold. But I don't think that'll be the takeaway. That's gonna be your one-way ticket to Rosencrantz. Oh my god, Aly! We need to be Rosencrantz and Gildenstern!"

Alison spaced out for a moment as she processed, missing the end of Paige's exclamation. "So, no gag, then?"

"No. No gags at all. Just you. You gotta trust yourself, Aly. You're good at this. Just, let the words carry you."

Alison was still dead from her dramatic flop. She rolled onto her back and put her hands behind her head. She nodded, but didn't respond. They shared a contemplative silence for a few moments before Paige erupted with something fresh.

"Oh! Aly! What about Edmund?"

"Edmund of Gloucester?"

"No, Edmund, the pastry chef who dreams of being an underwear designer. Yes, Edmund of Gloucester!"

Alison perked up at this. "Base, base, base?" she asked. Paige nodded. "What's the angle?"

"No angle, Aly," Paige responded. "It's just a strong role. Show them you– in a strong male role. Then, when you've already got the part of Hamlet, you can start adding all your funnies."

"Paige! I love it! Thank you!" They shared a sweet hug as Alison started to laugh maniacally, remembering bits of the speech. "Now Edmund the base shall top the legitimate!"

***

"Wildcard, this is Maverick. Do you read me? Over."

Alison sighed. "Yes, dear. The coms are operational. Also, I'm walking right next to you, so–"

"Sorry," Paige chirped through an embarrassed giggle. "I'm just excited. This is it. My first official mission."

They were heading north on Brook Street, staring down the immense postmodern glass of Prince Lab. This was Elephant Country: the Engineering Research Center attached at its south face, a tangled knot of concrete, glass, and steel with hard edges and clean lines. There was no good reason to loop around the campus in a nautilus pattern. Alison simply had the inclination to approach from the east, as it differed from her typical route. She had become accustomed to trusting her gut on these matters. *Good ol' gut. Metabolizing food and thinking critically since 1999.* Also, they were early and wanted to be late. Reed could sweat it out for a hot minute.

Alison put a hand on Paige's shoulder. "Okay, Paige. If you want to play with the coms, you can check in on Teddy Dalton. See if he's in position at the upper gallery of Pembroke."

"Jeeves, this is Maverick. Do you copy?"

Alison removed her hand from Paige's shoulder and executed an exasperated facepalm maneuver.

Dalton came in through the earpiece. "At the ready, miss."

"'Sir' will be fine, Jeeves."

"Very good, sir."

Paige was loving this dynamic. She knew she could count on an actor to follow the first rule of improv: always say yes. "I say, Jeeves. Are you in position?"

"Sir. I have arrived at the upper gallery. I have visual confirmation on operative Baker. By all accounts, he would appear to be alone. I shall ring to inform you of any changes, should they arise."

"Very good, Jeeves."

"Very good, sir."

Paige looked over at Alison to check the temperature on this new rogue element she had just thrown into the discourse. Her arms were folded, but she was smiling. Eye contact sparked a laugh from both of them. Their expressions snapped back to neutral under the gravity of the Pembroke Garden Maze as it entered their field of vision.

This part of campus was particularly lush: an amphitheatre cut into the trim, inclined lawn, lined with wide, semi-circular flower beds and low brick facades that followed the same lines. The grass was bathed in soft shade from nearby juniper and green ash and dotted with black railings and antique lamps. An old, wooden bench stood halfway up the incline, beneath the heavy, twisting boughs of a towering mossy oak. Approaching from behind, Alison could detect the faint outline of a well-manicured, ruby coif.

"Reed Baker," Alison said confidently as she circled. She landed at six o' clock, turned to face her rival, and sat cross-legged on the grass, leaving some clearance in case any funny business should arise. Paige stopped short and remained standing, arms folded, in an impatient pose.

"Alison, Paige," Reed replied, jovially. "Always a pleasure."

Paige said nothing, but took this opportunity to spit on the ground between them. Apparently, Reed Baker evoked the bad cop in her.

Alison was the first to break the lull left by the shocking gesture. "What have you got for us?"

"Ah," he returned. "Yes. Straight to brass tacks."

Paige erupted. "Are you patronizing me?"

"No, no. Just– keeping it light."

Paige flipped her first two fingers backwards against her opposing palm, cracking a single knuckle loudly. "I'll handle the mood lighting, bud. You can tell me what you and your Horsey Sauce pals have got cooked up. And it better be all the meats."

"Copy that." Reed began to unfold a campus map, smoothing it and placing it in the space between himself and Alison. "Here's Lyman. Leeds. Sharpe House. All Footman territory. We can have assets posted at Bio-Med, Granoff, and Green." He removed a handful of smooth, polished pebbles from his pocket, placing them at various positions on the map. We can each have an active operator, split channels if you like. Churchill House has a good lookout."

"I'd recommend against that," said Alison. "We lost a good operator on the upper deck of Churchill."

"Granoff, then. Now, if you've got six assets leaving the house at the same time, the Elephants would be wise to enter here, in the gangway between Sharpe and Peter Green. But, if there's a vantage point with eyes on all four positions, we can close the trap on any of these entrances."

"Oh!" chimed Paige. "What about the–"

Alison silenced her with a closed-hand gesture. "There is an ideal spot. We'll run our operator there. You take Granoff. We'll keep it clean for you."

"Great. We can afford to run four assets. You'll have six in play?"

"Four," said Alison, "when it comes to the fighting. We'll have all six move on the sortie. Four will loop around here, at Lippitt House, and join you for the fight."

"What if they have GPS on you?"

"We intend for them to be tracking us. We'll hand off our phones at Lippitt and have the remaining two assets proceed, with the whole stack, to the secondary objective."

"Hm," Reed reflected. "So, you're going to leak a real mission? Not a false flag?"

"Yes," said Alison, folding her fingers together. "We'll act on intelligence provided by you."

Reed brought his hand to his chin, covering his mouth partially with his first finger. His eyebrows furrowed in a way that simultaneously provoked infatuation and enmity as he thought about the proposition. "I might have something for you." He produced his phone and started scrolling methodically, returning the trio to a state of silence for a beat.

Paige lost patience first. "Has anybody ever just slapped you out of the blue?"

His eyes remained fixed on his screen. "Not to my knowledge. Why do you ask?"

"You have a very slappable face."

Reed smiled politely. "I'm going to take that as a compliment. Ah, here we are. Have a look at these doofuses." He tossed the phone over to Alison. Paige shifted behind her and bent down to look over her shoulder.

"Yikes," Alison said as she started scrolling through the images. An asset was affixing college pins on two fraternity pledges, a Sigma Alpha Epsilon insignia clearly visible in the background. "What faction is this?"

Reed gave a confident half-smile. "From what we can tell, Chariot. That's Danny Ross in the pullover."

Paige jumped in here. "But why post it on Instagram?"

"Hard to say," Reed replied. "But my guess is bait. They want to lure assets into the SAE house."

"Okay, Reed. I like this for a multi-asset mission. But we're not walking into a trap."

"That's reasonable. You need more control over the venue. Might I suggest–" He reached out for the phone and Alison returned it to him, at which time he scrolled up a few images on the Sigma House Instagram page. He gave another collected smile and handed the phone off again.

A gaudy cartoon of a chicken, pig, and cow, dancing

before a bonfire in Acapulco shirts filled the screen. Paige read the headline over Alison's shoulder. "Tenth Annual Sigma Alpha Epsilon Three Kinds of Meat Cookout."

"Hm," pondered Alison. "Outdoor venue. Big crowd. Multiple exits. Let me see that map." She traced her finger from the hand-off at Lippitt House to the Sigma Alpha Epsilon Fraternity House on East Angell. "It's a straight shot. Paige?"

Paige took a few glances back and forth between the phone and the map, then studied Reed's slappable face for signs of deceit. "I think we can make it work."

Alison tossed Reed's phone back to him. He slipped it in his pocket and extended his pale hand to shake. "Okay," he said.

"Okay," Alison repeated, shaking his hand and stealing a glance into his warm, hazel eyes. As per usual, they offered her that strange cocktail of butterflies and rage. Paige broke the spell, looping her arm through the crook of Alison's elbow and helping her to her feet. They were long past the apex of the Pembroke gardens when Reed finished packing his bag.

***

Paige returned to her coms as they rounded the corner of Meeting Street and Grant. "Did you get all that, Jeeves?"

"Quite, sir. Most illuminating."

"What do you make of it?"

"Well, sir. I must give the young master credit for one thing."

Paige borrowed a moment of eye contact with her compatriot before continuing. "And what's that, Jeeves?"

"It would appear he was most capable of delivering all the meats."

SIX

"No!" shouted Alison, sternly, and much louder than she had expected. "I have already told you no. And stop looking at me like that! Every time we come to this juncture, you give me that look. It was no before and it's still no. Give it up, already."

Alison's one pair of yoga pants offered no reply. She was preparing for a run, to get out some nervous energy. It was getting colder. October offered no solace to New Haven. She would have to be cold: her prejudice against this garment was too strong. "It's not you, it's me." She settled on a pair of burgundy shorts with an understated college seal and small lettering that read "Women's Crew." Alison did not know this, but the Bauer College Women's Crew Team exclusively wore yoga pants. This mystery would be kept from her for her entire tenure at Bauer, for there are some things that each person simply must not know.

She had about an hour to kill before Peters posted the Hamlet cast list on the interior double-doors of the Lyman Hall Great Room. Running for an hour was, of course, a hard no– but she could drag it out. Make it a whole production. A nice armament scene. The camera could zoom in on her electric blue Asics as she pulled closed the laces. One of those showers where you lean an arm against the opposing wall and just stand there, hunched over like a maniac. Even if it were January, this would be time for a run. Unable to cast Hamlet herself, Alison had no control over the outcome. No control meant severe discomfort, and typically some externalization. Running was all hers. She chose the pace, she chose the route. She could even dishonor gods by making no offering to the temple of Lululemon.

The cold hit her like a sack of Siberian potatoes, and she immediately went to her phone to arrange some intrinsic motivation with Silversun Pickups. There was no internal struggle on this one. She went straight for the hard stuff: Bloody Mary. The effervescent guitars and pulsing break beat sent a jolt of electricity through Alison, and she settled into a long gait. The sweet, harmonic drones lulled her into a hypnotic state as she flew down Court towards the main drag. The rising chorus exploded into a fireball, starting from the base of her spine, delivering warm fireflies all the way to her fingertips.

The opening lyric to the next track, Busy Bees, always provoked a wry laugh from Alison. Today, it snapped her out of a dreary trance. *Wait. Did I just listen to that whole album twice?* A pool of sweat at the base of her neck confirmed her suspicion. A quick u-turn, and she was back on Meeting Street to prepare for her day and the inevitable divining of her fate. From the corner of her eye, she caught a glimpse of a vaguely familiar figure tucking itself out of sight behind the marble facade of the Emery Building. She was overtaken by a strong sense of déjà vu as she looped around West House and headed home. She shook it off for the moment, as more pressing matters awaited, but placed a tiny fold in the corner of the page in her memory where long, brown coats resided.

She had had the good sense to turn her ringer off, and a quick glance at the screen revealed two new voicemails and three texts. She didn't need to look to be certain that the list was up, and dear Paige had comments. She in fact made a point of not looking. She'd like to see the list in person, thanks very much. Ignoring the blinking green light of the world, Alison took her time getting to that godforsaken cast list. She imagined Paige trying to read it out to her as she drowned out all sound with the blow dryer. She even took her breakfast seated at the dining room table for the first time this year, foregoing her typical walk-and-eat methodology.

But the time did finally arrive when Alison would burst dramatically into the Great Hall and see the extent of the damage. As soon as she was close enough to read the names, she closed her eyes instinctively, like she was staring down a barreling semi truck and bracing for impact. Maybe she could just stop time right now. Or slow it to a crawl. Live an entire lifetime in her mind's eye before facing what reality lay behind the protective curtain of her eyelids. She could be a modest cabbage farmer. Take a simple husband named Jeremy Wallace. Have two sons. Paul and Davey. *Oh, Davey. Always getting into the peanut butter jar. You'll spoil your supper, Davey!*

"How 'bout that!" sang a honey baritone behind her. *Dang.* She thought she'd at least get to see her first grandchild before shuffling off her mortal coil. *Ah, well. There's the respect that makes calamity of so long life.*

"How 'bout that," she repeated, opening her eyes and trying to play catch-up on what that was and what she might make of it. She placed the voice before her eyes could focus on the list in front of her. It was Casey Harrington.

Casey was the poster-boy for every manifestation of privilege that New England society had laid out on its showroom floor. The first son of a powerful shipping mogul with ties to James Fisk himself, Casey attended Bauer on a sailing scholarship. Notwithstanding the rather essential intelligence that none of his contemporaries in the theatre department had ever seen him so much as lower a jib, he integrated the seafaring motif deeply into his persona. He wore slacks, and possessed more garments featuring anchors than a Delta Gamma sister– though, admittedly, his were more subtle. He even had a blue jacket with brass buttons. If he were wearing it today, Alison would not have been able to resist the urge to rip off a handful of brass buttons and force-feed them to him. It should also be mentioned that in addition to his wealth and easy charm, Casey Harrington was classically handsome. Square-jawed and dusted with a sweeping, golden mantle, he could wear a snowsuit and still look like a shirtless Abercrombie model.

Alison's eyes came into focus and immediately noticed his name at the top of the list, adjacent to the name Hamlet. The Balkan potato sack returned, this time as an anchor tied in a perfect clove hitch to the mainsail of her sinking heart. She stood in silence, a clock ticking in the back of her head to remind her of her basic social obligations. Soon, she'd have to congratulate this thieving magpie who had just made off with her prize-winning pig. *That from a shelf the precious diadem stole, and put it in his pocket. A king of shreds and patches!* But now, for the life of her, Alison couldn't even find her own name.

Another run from top to bottom revealed that Paige Hall would be playing the role of Horatio. *Good for her! Now where the blazes is Alison Ashe?* An eternity later, or after at least enough time to see young Davey drive off to his first prom, she found it. It was at the very bottom of the page. "Understudy for Ophelia: Alison Ashe." And then, in pencil, "See me." Her brain rattled off a thousand voracious curses, but her mouth could only produce a single "Fff," which Casey mistook for exhaling anyway.

"Looks like we'll be spending some time together," he said, the essence of middle-school-boy bleeding out of him like a can of Axe body spray with a severed cap. Alison was aware that there was a wellspring of theatre majors who would relish the opportunity to practice kissing Casey Harrington. To Alison, the prospect offered only sea-sickness. Maybe if she could actually play Ophelia, this shipwreck would be salvageable. But as a just-in-case Ophelia, the Casey factor only added insult to injury.

Again, Alison came to the realization that it was her turn to talk. She was working on a nautical pun warning him not to do anything that would provoke her to kick him in the dinghy, but all that came out was "Uh huh." To send the point home, she followed up with a long silence, somewhere in the middle of which she realized her jaw had been wide open for enough time to co-sign Davey's first mortgage.

"Good talk," he said, patting her awkwardly on the shoulder and escaping stage left.

"Now I am alone," she said quietly to the cast list when

Casey had cleared the starboard end of the hall. "O, what a rogue and peasant slave am I."

***

Alison didn't like to hold onto melancholy for very long. She much preferred the proactive approach of pounding on doors and demanding answers. To her chagrin, Peters's door was already wide open when she finished her grimacing death march and approached his office. She briefly considered slamming it shut so she could blast it open again with a battering ram, but lacked both the proper inclination and equipment. The small office was flooded with well-loved books, keepsakes, and posters from old horror films. Two chairs faced his modest teak desk. By the time Alison had barged in and plopped luxuriously into the first, she noticed that the far chair was occupied as well. She kicked both feet onto the professor's desk before looking over to find Annie Watts, whom she recalled would be playing the real Ophelia.

"Two Ophelias diverged in a yellow wood," Alison exclaimed as she settled in.

"Alison, welcome," replied Peters.

Annie offered a little wave. "Hey, Aly! I was just asking Professor Peters about the production design."

"And I was just telling her that we'll have to negotiate that with the Technical Theatre majors. They're the ones who really get to see their visions through. I'm just the old fussbudget who says when to stop and go."

"Old fussbudget?" Annie interjected, incredulous.

"Now, now, Annie," Alison chimed. "We mustn't placate him. He wants you to tell him that thirty-nine isn't old.

Resist the low-hanging fruit. Peters, you're as old as you feel. If you feel like an old fussbudget, then you be the best old fussbudget you can be!"

"Okay, dear," returned Annie. "Can I still give him shade for using the word fussbudget?"

"You can. He may not even catch your shade, though. The man's a grade-A fussbudget, after all."

Peters threw up his arms in defeat. "These words like daggers enter into mine ears."

Annie stood and started gathering her coat and backpack, a smile still lingering from Alison's infectious charm. "Think I'll be off, then. Thanks for the talk, prof."

Alison scrunched her legs into her chest to give clearance for Annie's exit. Still in egg-form, she gave Annie a little kick. "Do me a favor and don't get the plague. I don't wanna have Cap'n Crunch trying to plunder my treasures in front of a live audience."

"Ew!" she replied. "Girl, get thee to a nunnery!"

When Annie was long gone, Alison snapped into a serious expression, folded her fingers, and leaned forward menacingly. "Okay, bud. Spill."

Peters shifted. "We both know you're a fine actor, Alison."

"Well, I'm no Annie Watts, but–"

"Apples and oranges, kid. Not even relevant to your paradigm. But, I get it. In this business, we're always comparing ourselves to our contemporaries."

Alison gave this some thought. "Yeah, it's not healthy. We're like moths to a self-loathing flame."

"Quite," noted Peters, regaining his train of thought. "Alison, I believe you have untapped potential that transcends stagecraft."

Alison nodded, growing tired of the vague preamble. "What is it?"

"I want you to take on the role of Fight Director for Hamlet."

"Hm," she mused. "Okay, yeah, I get that I have a proclivity for stage combat."

"Alison, it's more than that. You're a prodigy."

Alison felt awkward accepting compliments, especially from credible sources. She tucked a sneaker under a spare leg and considered. "But, I won't get practicum credit."

"Well, not for the Repertory Program–" countered Peters.

"You want me to change majors?" Alison exclaimed, raising her voice in shock.

Professor Peters removed a file from his desk drawer and opened it. It was Alison's transcript. She had never actually seen it in person. Courses on the left, a web of numbered cells on the right, filled exclusively with fours. Alison wouldn't risk a B in college. It felt like a wasted investment. Besides, she was fully aware that someday she'd be on the hook to support her mother. This visual representation of her excellence thus far was heartening.

"You've actually taken a fair share of the requisite Theatre Tech classes. I know you were planning on a low-impact senior year. But if you take a full course load, you should still be able to graduate on schedule."

Alison was puzzled. "It seems wasteful. I mean– It's still a BFA in Theatre Arts, just a different specialization. Why would I do all that extra work?"

"You're already registered as a Combatant with the Society of American Fight Directors. If you complete this practicum, and pass the SAFD Fight Director Test, I can offer you a fellowship in our MFA program."

"You can what?"

"I can offer you an MFA fellowship in Technical Theatre, with a specialization in Fight Directing. That means we pay you to continue your studies here. And you'll teach Stage Combat One. Dr. Foster is running out of steam."

Alison suddenly felt the room's gravity triple. "That's a three-year commitment! I was just getting used to the idea of graduating. This is– this is a lot to take in."

"I understand," said Peters. "Give it some thought. I can't re-cast Hamlet, but you've paid your dues. If you want to stay in-company, you'll probably get a lead next season. But keep in mind, the industry isn't kind to actors. Even the good ones. An MFA in Theatre Tech from Bauer is a skeleton key to Broadway, if you don't mind being out of the spotlight. You pass the test for Fight Master, and you'll be a heck of a commodity."

"Okay, okay," she volleyed, overwhelmed. "This is too much to process right now. Let me get back to you– next week?"

"Take your time, Alison."

"Okay," she replied, compressing her coat into a little ball in her arms. "I'll let you know when I make a decision– you fussbudget."

***

All three texts and one of the voicemails were from Paige, who was ready to tear down Lyman Hall brick by brick to protest the travesty of casting Aly as an understudy. The other voicemail was from her mother. Though they were quite close, Alison's mom gave her a lot of space, especially in college. She only texted sporadically, and Alison couldn't recall a single phone call they had shared while classes were in session. Standing in the lower stairwell, she immediately pulled up the message.

"Hey, Aly. It's mom. Just checking in. How are you? Did you try out for Hamlet? You'd make such a beautiful Ophelia. Anyway, I miss you. Oh, my– um, Humana isn't covering my brand of insulin anymore, and I'm allergic to one of the ingredients in the one they do cover. So, I'm going to see if I can get more hours at work. If not, I think I can get by. Just– just letting you know I won't be as available. Anyway, if you want to come down one weekend, I'd love to have lunch with you. Love you, sweetie. Bye."

Irene Ashe was a pharmacy tech at her neighborhood CVS. Having spent her whole life managing her own life-threatening illness, her overwhelming optimism blinded her to the irony of spending long hours handling and processing this life-saving drug for others, when its availability to herself was under threat. She was also fairly obstinate when it came to accepting help, especially from her daughter. Alison would have to find a way to covertly transfer some extra funds to her mother, and that also probably meant a few more hours a month slinging artisanal gin to mustachioed man-children.

The gravity-well of the day's events sent her into a macabre waltz as she struggled to walk home against its crippling weight. She dragged her feet uneasily past the dreary, leafless cottonwoods of West Court, entranced by the soothing haze of a thick, rolling fog.

Only then, when her eyelids were in deep, sullen descent, and the halcyon mists of sleep had begun washing over her weary frame, did she catch a second glimpse of a long, brown coat.

SEVEN

"Thirty minutes."

"Thank you, thirty."

Surely an advantage of the Lord Chamberlain's Men could be observed in their well-established lines and methods of communication. Stagecraft, as they saw it, shared a number of the fundamental characteristics and imperatives of tradecraft. A production required tightly coordinated efforts from experts in a range of fields. It demanded creativity, delegation, and trust. From first-read to opening night, anything short of a well-oiled machine could cascade into disaster. And even then, as a great fussbudget once said, "Fifty things will go wrong." It was up to the actors and crew to improvise and make adjustments, and do so seamlessly enough that the audience failed to notice. At Bauer, the methodology was simple: give the actors a strong toolkit and let them choose how it might be used. Peters especially avoided detailed blocking. He preferred to offer students methods for establishing clarity in movement, and let the blocking happen organically.

It occurred to Alison that this too was the modus operandi behind the tradecraft of The Lord Chamberlain's Men. Assets learned simple tenets in training, but had agency in how they might apply them in the field. She considered this congruence as she sat patiently with Paige under the blue-gelled worklight of the Leeds Hall lighting booth, going over the logistics of the joint operation that lay ahead that evening. Paige sat too, but not patiently. She squirmed and fidgeted with the toggles of her coat, following the lines of the map nervously with her finger as they ran over possible complications.

"Can you go over the five tenets again?"

"Paige, you know the tenets."

"I know, but it calms me down to hear you say them."

"Fine," Alison surrendered. "I suppose it can't hurt to keep the basics on the front page, especially considering the complexity of our op tonight."

"Thank you."

"I got you, pumpkin. One. Focus. Every detail counts."

"Right," Paige said, recalling the simple, concise prose. "Follow the patterns, watch for deviations. No coincidences."

"Good. Two. Clear the cobwebs."

"Try to quell the fog of emotions. Letting them take root can breed mistakes."

Alison nodded. "Three. Find the words. You can talk your way out of a bad situation more easily than you can fight your way out."

Paige smiled. "We can agree to disagree on that one."

"Four. Relinquish control. You can't control all the factors in every situation. The sooner you know this, the sooner you can adapt."

"But the gods will be caught looking if Alison Ashe doesn't try." Paige was already in a better mood.

Alison gave a friendly scowl. "Okay, dumpling. What's the last one?"

Paige raised an index finger. "Find absolution. If you can empathize with your enemy, you can think like your enemy."

"Twenty minutes," Teddy Dalton's calm, patient voice sang through the coms.

"Thank you, twenty," repeated the chorus of Lord Chamberlain's Men, stationed at various positions scattered throughout Footman territory.

Weeks of meticulous preparation prefaced this evening's enterprise. The business of purposefully leaking an intricate operation without divulging true intent was a delicate game, and the Footmen were careful and deliberate in their means and methods. Alison's phone had already been compromised by Elephant operatives, an oversight from a previous operation that she would come to cleverly leverage into an advantage. It would serve as the seed, through which she and her allies could pick and choose what intelligence would be exposed, and when. A series of carefully-timed communications painted a clear picture of this evening's sortie, right up to the point of the switch, when all of the Lord Chamberlain's mobiles would be transferred to two active operatives, who would carry out a Dolly Dagger on Sigma House while the rest circled back to seal the trap on any encroaching Elephants. Cavalry assets had agreed to take postings in the vicinity, and a single night's armistice was agreed upon between themselves and the Footmen, in order that they might optimize the damage potential against a common enemy.

In order to ensure smooth coordination between

factions, Operative Reed Baker was patched in, for this evening only, to Lord Chamberlain's open com channel.

"This is Operative Baker, just checking in. How's everything going on your end?"

"I'm sorry," Paige exclaimed, excitable as ever. "We don't know an Operative Baker. Do you have a call sign that might help us identify you?"

A sigh could be heard on the line, followed by a sizable pause. "Do I have to?"

"Sorry stranger. Rules are rules." Paige was grinning wildly.

Another sigh, another pause. "This is Strawberry Pompadour. Do you copy?"

"That's a ten-four, Pompadour. How are things looking on Ice Cream Mountain?"

Alison gave Paige a little smack in the ribs and whispered "Jesus, babe. You're gonna break him."

"All assets are in position. Our operator has found a strong vantage point at Granoff. He's running the show from there. I'll serve as liaison on our end. I take it you two will do the same?"

"That's right," Alison spoke up. "Have you spotted any movement?"

Reed cleared his throat. "We're seeing a few telltale signs of reconnaissance on the Sharpe-Green side of the territory. You might want to send an asset to make a sweep down Olive. Make sure they get the message that it's on."

"What do you think, Butler?"

Ed Butler's deep voice was easily distinguishable above the crowd. "That's near my position. And I see no harm in it. I'll make the sweep."

"Boffo," said Paige, a smile in her voice. "Thanks for the sit-rep, shortcake. Do keep us posted if anything changes."

"Copy that."

At the ten minute mark– "Thank you, ten"– Alison and Paige packed their effects, donned their coats, fastened various buttons, and pulled tightly on backpack straps. Paige wore a drab green fishtail parka with a fur-lined hood, and ran the lines of her coms and phone from its interior pocket. Alison never wore a coat that wasn't grey. Tonight, she had equipped a canvas military jacket, lined with a hoodie three shades darker. Her white earbud cord draped in front of her cable-knit sweater before twisting around to her back pocket. While the Elephants had recently upgraded to a practically invisible wireless system, The Lord Chamberlain's Men preferred tried-and-true headphones, cables and all. Upon request, Andy McElroy had outfitted Alison and Paige with quarter-inch splitters, enabling them to use their coms and listen to music simultaneously. Although they thanked him profusely, he maintained that the credit belonged to the nice man at Radio Shack.

At five minutes– "Thank you, five"– Alison undid the laces of her shoes and re-laced them tightly, crouching in what she felt was a cool pose as she worked.

"Aly, whatcha doing?" asked Paige, confusion pressing gently at her left eyebrow.

"It's for the montage."

"Montage?"

"Yeah– in my head. Don't question my methods!"

"Places," crooned Teddy Dalton once more through the coms.

"Thank you, places."

***

Six theatre majors exited a small rehearsal hall on the north face of Sharpe House, still buzzing after a clamorous run-through of Words, Words, Words by David Ives. They laughed with great gusto, quoting lines from the show as they turned south on Grant towards Waterman. They were headed to Sigma House for a party. Although theatre majors typically kept their distance from fraternities, Greek Life at Bauer was more reserved than at other colleges, making cross-pollination more feasible. This party in particular had more draws than turn-offs. It was located in Sigma's beautifully lit garden, grilled meats were promised in abundance, and proceeds went to childhood cancer research. One of the students at the head of the pack carried a small flyer which read "Partake in many meats, cancer we'll defeat."

If ever an olive branch existed between the sentiments of fraternities and theatre majors, it was unequivocally rooted in puns.

As the rowdy gang approached Lippitt House, one of the students stopped, garnering the attention of his companions. "Does anyone wanna go back to the dorms and drop off their bags?"

A few takers voiced their approval. A small-framed girl with bright features and a green parka asserted that she'd rather press on. Her taller friend in grey did the same. Hugs were exchanged, and the party broke up there, heading in opposite directions.

The conversation took on a quieter, more personal tone as Alison and Paige strolled east on Waterman Street, whose aged, opalescent cobblestones were illuminated by moonlight and soft yellow lamps.

Alison spoke first. "What did you end up doing for your Hamlet paper?"

The question brought a twinge of Machiavellian delight to Paige's expression. "Oh, I– um. I argued that Hamlet was a work of feminist literature."

"You what? Do you really believe that?"

"No! Not even a little bit. Not even a smidge. There are no smidges of feminism in Hamlet."

Alison gave a look of incredulity, a smile embedded beneath. "Then what did you–" She left the question unfinished.

"I just kind of riffed. Blah, blah, Lady Gertrude, matriarch. Blah, blah, Ophelia, death as an escape from the dominant narrative. The angle wasn't the argument itself."

"What was it, then?"

Paige gave that impish look again. "It was mostly just a bunch of rhetorical traps that Peters wouldn't want to engage with. It was the essay equivalent of 'Does this dress make me look fat?'"

"Spicy! So, what did you get?"

"An A minus."

"Should have been a C minus. To mirror our seventy cents on the dollar."

Paige laughed. "How poor are they that have not patience? What wound did ever heal but by degrees?"

Alison Ashe put her arm around Paige's shoulder as the garden lights of Sigma House appeared in the distance. The coms were starting to light up. Status reports became more heightened. Movement was spotted, enemy operatives identified. The telltale heavy breathing and pounding footfalls of assets in play. Alison could see that the radio activity was doing a number on Paige's demeanor.

"Let's switch to a private channel," she said after a tentative breath. "At this point, we've gotta trust that our boys can do their jobs. Besides, we've got our own work to do, too. You wanna sync our playlists? You got the one I sent you?" Paige nodded the affirmative. "Okay. At Night in Dreams, by White Denim, in three, two–"

The wild, euphoric guitar riff and loose, funky drums imbued both operatives with confident smirks and rhythmic footfalls. They exchanged a dry look in the pale light before bursting into beautiful, sardonic laughter. Alison had never felt more at home than she did in that moment, wrapped cozily in the warm blanket of that riotous laugh. Paige's unabashed snort sealed the deal. Whatever happened that night didn't matter. This was a lifelong friendship. And nothing could take that from her. By the chorus, they were bleeding self-assurance like Tom Cruise on stilts.

The front entrance to Sigma Alpha Epsilon was dark. Lighted signs pointed the way around black pike fencing to the rear gate. The massive garden looked to Alison to be emblazoned with otherworldly magic: a thousand will o' wisps dancing across its well-groomed grounds. The frat boys went overboard with the lights. String lights ran the gauntlet from the upper-balcony down to the far fences below. Box lanterns floated about the perimeter, and hundreds of drop lights fell from the ancient weeping willows. The party was already packed, and newcomers continued to trickle in from all directions, a pilgrimage to the city of lights.

As advertised, it was also the city of meats. Three great grills were elevated on a high central platform, manned by three mighty grill-masters. These exalted paragons operated their altars with expert focus, shirtless but for their bonny golden aprons, each adorned with the Sigma House Seal. Perhaps to further their ascent to godhood, they wore soft laurels in their hair. As pilgrims wandered toward the altar, they were blessed with the spoils wrought from hoof and feather. Bless their freshly-waxed chests and their humble hearts beneath, they'd done it. For there were three kinds of meat.

"What now?" asked Paige, still enchanted by the gratuitous decor.

"Now, we work the party, Moneypenny," replied Alison. She had been saving that one.

They made their way to the bar, where a flaxen beefcake mixed them each a cocktail of their choosing. Neither intended to get sloshed, but they deemed that a drink in hand would ease their navigation of the complex social structures inherent in a frat party. For the sake of expert record-keeping it should be noted that Paige ordered an Old Fashioned and Alison selected a Gin Rickey. That is until they switched, for Alison's drink was "gross," and she had only ordered it because it sounded cool. Before the evening's business could be conducted, it was also imperative that they each sampled all the meats. You know. For the kids.

"So, we're keeping an eye out for these faces," Alison said quietly to Paige, her phone open to the Sigma House Instagram page. "That's Danny Ross in the rugby shirt.

Senior. The two pledges: we think they're Mike Rivers and Jesse Flores."

Without removing her eyes from the phone, Paige replied "Well, the first one's easy. He's been on the balcony the whole time."

Alison didn't want to draw attention either. She turned her body a few degrees to the left and flipped off the display to her phone, trying to find the balcony in its reflection. Danny Ross stood still at its guardrail like a sentry, quietly scanning the party below. *Hm*, thought Alison. *This is going to require some finesse.*

Both assets shifted their positions again, subtly, but enough to keep their backs between their college pins and Danny's sightlines. "Paige, pull up your Insta. We need to see if either of the pledges have girlfriends." Mike did. Madison Miller. Jet black hair, emerald eyes, with a telltale headband to bring them out. Paige spotted her under one of the willows, hunched over a phone with a friend, just as she and Alison were. Maybe she was planning a hit job tonight as well.

"Madison? Madison Miller?" Alison asked timidly as they approached, still trying to keep their backs to the balcony. Madison looked up from her phone, no signs of recognition in her face. She widened her eyes to answer in the affirmative, but didn't speak.

"We're friends of Mike's," Paige took over. "from Lake High." Golly, she was good. "I'm Stacy, and this is Becks. He was so excited to introduce you to us tonight, but we can't find him."

"Oh, snap! Yeah, they put him on waiter duty tonight. He's been roaming around with little toothpick wieners. But, yeah, it's so nice to meet you!"

"You too! We've heard so much about you! Hey, do you happen to know Jesse Flores?"

"Yeah, he's staying in tonight. He got completely wasted last night. Probably still yakking up there."

"Dang," Alison chimed. "That sucks. Stacy, you wanna loop around and find Mike? We need to tell him that he found a keeper. Madison, it was so nice to meet you!"

"Gosh, you too!"

Alison and Paige made a serpentine path to a picnic table whose purview was blocked by the Altar of Meats. Hunched over a phone, they studied a campus map that Alison had pulled up from the My Bauer app. A small breeze rolled in, causing the drop lights and box lanterns to sway. Shadows danced on the rosewood table before them as they recalculated the mission.

"What do you think?" Paige asked, after Alison had bit her lip in silence for a fair moment.

"I think we shouldn't get too greedy. I don't like Danny on the balcony. He hasn't moved an inch since we first spotted him. There's an easy mark in the house. Let's finish him off and get out of here. Can you play operator out here while I make the play?"

"What? Aly, we're not supposed to go into Sigma House. It's a trap!"

"If it is a trap, they're shorthanded tonight. And you can keep me informed on movements in and out of the house." Paige twisted her face, but nodded reluctantly in agreement. "Besides," Alison continued, "I like doing things I'm not supposed to."

EIGHT

Hands in pockets, whiskey abandoned on polished rosewood, Alison left the city of lights. The stark contrast of the darkened front facade looked ominous under the pale moon. A black, wrought iron gate with pike-topped tines barred entrance to the eastern face of the house, where she hoped to find quiet passage. She tried to take in as much of the scene as possible without breaking stride. A passerby wouldn't take kindly to some rando hulking up a tree and plopping over the gate, even when accounting for typical fraternity shenanigans. It also occurred to Alison that this was her second count of breaking and entering this term, and that her explanation to Johnny Law, should he come a' knocking, would be that it was for a fun game. *Officer, I was just going in there to assault a sick Freshman. I mean, he's a pledge, so, he knew the risks. You wanna let me off with a warning?*

"Wildcard, this is Maverick, do you copy?"

"Paige, are you having separation anxiety? It's been, like, thirty seconds."

Paige paused for a beat. "Okay, not fair. Of course I miss you, boo! Anyway, I was just thinking, maybe we need to establish a panic button. Like, a code word we can say if things go sideways and you need an extraction."

Alison smiled, her face still twisted in thought as she tried to envision a path over the gate. "Uh huh. How about 'I need an extraction?'"

"You wanna say that right in front of an enemy asset? You want to tell a combatant that backup is on the way?"

"Okay, okay. You have a point. If I'm ever in trouble, I will say–" She considered this for a moment before the answer settled on her mind like a memory, rather than an invention. "Jellybean."

"Then it's settled."

Alison made a quick perimeter check before dashing into a full sprint towards a sycamore whose branches draped over the nearby gate. Two steps up the trunk and she launched herself toward a midsection branch. She grappled the branch with both hands and used the momentum to hoist her body over the gate, arching her back as she crossed the threshold in Fosbury Flop position. She stumbled hard on the landing, but she was on the other side. A sharp twinge of pain revealed that she had earned a sizable gash on her left ankle from one of the defending pikes. She smiled a little at her red badge of courage as she made her way stealthily through the brambles by Sigma's eastern face.

Three sets of white garden doors offset the red brick exterior of the wing. She tried each set. Locked. There were two balconies, but no obvious handholds to gain passage towards them, save for a precarious drainage gutter. A quick scan revealed an open window on the south balcony. The gutter, however, had other plans, tapering down at an angle that limited accessibility to the north balcony alone. She'd have to cross that bridge when she came to it. One foot on a nearby water spout, she thrust her body upward toward the gutter. It dug uncomfortably into her hands, but failed to break the skin. From her dead hang, she noticed her breathing quickening. Nerves, she thought, but reevaluated as it got even heavier, incorporating a low rumble into each exhale. *Am I wheezing?*

She wasn't. Another perimeter check conceded the presence of an enormous English Bulldog. Sporting coarse grey hide and a spiked collar, he had a mean grimace and a heavy stride. Make no mistake: this was an absolute unit. The chunk-de-resistance. Marky Mark and the Chunky Bunch. He trotted towards her as she dangled like a rotisserie chicken. Apparently, there were four types of meat available tonight. Alison remained motionless as the guard dog approached, a silver tag dangling from his collar. She strained to see the name on the tag as a low growl emerged from his heinous muzzle. It read "Spork."

The rumbling ceased momentarily, ostensibly to precipitate the sounding of alarm. But what followed was not a thunderous bark, but another sound entirely. To Alison, it resembled the sound of a child eating a banana: a hearty, moist smack. And then, another. Further reconnaissance revealed that young Spork was catching droplets of blood emanating from her ankle. The wound was worse than she initially gauged. Blood had soaked clean through her high tops and was apparently delivering a jackpot of forbidden delicacy to the interested party below. She took the win, sidling up toward the north balcony as her fuzzy Roomba followed eagerly underfoot. Finally, she was up and over the railing.

The clearance to the opposing balcony looked to be about five feet. Alison scoured her mind for the last time she had done a long jump, and whether this was even a remotely possible endeavor. The gap seemed to widen as she evaluated, her head filling with static as images of her imminent peril flickered past. Her breathing quickened and her heart pounded, the world around her blurring and darkening as a lightheaded film enveloped her senses.

Focus.

And reality snapped back into place. Two quick steps and a hearty leap saw her over the gap, albeit with a hard landing and a pulse of pain as her hip crashed hard into the opposing railing. She had started on the window, slowly and quietly lifting its lower frame when the low rumble returned– this time with an expectant whimper. She took a moment to appraise Spork's demeanor. Though she had never had a dog herself, she knew the precursors of excitable barking. If she slipped through the window now, that was that. But she couldn't bring herself to bail either. Frozen in indecision, caught between a Spork and a hard place, Alison let out a long, thoughtful breath, and let the words float into her consciousness.

Clear the cobwebs.

It came to her with a burst of overwhelming, lucid clarity. The gods required an offering. Lowering herself into a crouching position, she undid the knot and pulled loose the laces from her bloody All Stars. The charcoal Chuck had accepted the crimson pigment, giving off a new purplish hue of plum sauce or a cheap Pinot. The sopping sneaker made an obscene squish as it popped off her heel, a violent mist of blood splattering on her face and clothes in the jolt. An eager tail wagged impatiently below. The shoe tumbled bleakly downward, a macabre harbinger of cruel fate, until it was enthusiastically caught in the beast's fervent maw. Alison ditched the other shoe as well, hoping to avoid an awkward gait in the mission ahead. She slipped through the open window, glancing back momentarily to see dear Spork disappear into the bushes with his prize. It occurred to her that she may have just negotiated the most amicable consensus in diplomatic history.

The interior was more posh than Alison expected, though she had little time to admire the mid-century modern design of the Sigma House bedrooms while trying to bleed her way quietly through its floorplan. She slinked toward the door facing the upper level hallway and performed a head check, smirking acerbically at how quiet her movement had become in her socks. She nearly jumped out of them when Paige came in through the coms.

"Hey, honeydew. Looks like you've got company."

"Rugby shirt?"

"Yeah. He looked a little bored and turned in toward the main house. Probably a routine sweep. I wouldn't worry. He's on the second floor."

"I'm on the second floor!" Alison gritted through her teeth as a wave of nervous energy tightened her muscles and shortened her breath. "What do I do?"

"Don't get caught."

Alison's first inclination was to try a rushing play. Charge down the hall, wind up, haymaker. Maybe she could catch him sleeping. However, having seen the asset in question, she wasn't sure she could even make a dent. Danny Ross was built like a rhinoceros that played for the

Oakland A's. In the eighties. She could hear his footsteps starting down the other end of the long hallway, stopping to check rooms as he passed them. Whatever she was going to do, she had to do it sooner than later.

Find the words.

In all the commotion, it hadn't occurred to Alison until this moment that her playlist was still on. The song that had just begun, however, couldn't be ignored. It was William Shatner and Ben Folds, covering Pulp's Common People. Folds had arranged the music: it was a catchy, upbeat, guitar-laden affair. Power chords surged over heavy, grungy drums; the whole mix was loud and full of wild energy. Shatner delivered the lyrics in spoken word over the music. It was preposterously bizarre, and Alison loved every second of it. When she had put it on her Heist Playlist, she couldn't offer a good defense for its presence. Now, not only did it jostle her out of her paralysis, it gave her an idea.

She reached into her bag for one of the Lord Chamberlain's cell phones she had picked up in the exchange earlier, immediately recognizing it as Teddy Dalton's. With her own phone, she dialed Teddy's number. She answered quickly with the extraneous phone, put it on speaker, and cranked the volume. A quick peek into the antechamber revealed that Rugby Ross still had distance to cover before arriving at her juncture. Alison slid the phone as hard as she could under the opposite-facing bedroom door and, hiding behind a trophy case in the hallway, blasted her favorite William Shatner recording through its surprisingly resonant speaker.

Danny Ross was on it like a bulldog on a bloody loafer.

He barreled down the hallway, swinging his arms in power-walking formation. Alison took the opportunity to tiptoe past, under the audible smokescreen of Danny's violent door-opening methods. While protocol demands restraint from looking back in these tense maneuvers, Alison couldn't help but steal a peek at his very confused face as he confronted an invisible but spirited Captain Kirk in the midst of a rebellious punk phase. This would have been a fine time for Danny to drop to his knees for an overhead shot while shouting the names of his enemies, but Alison would have to clear the hallway before she could start writing that scene into the screenplay.

She continued to sneak down the hallway with only the subtlest hint of squish beneath her sodded sock, when a spiral staircase appeared to the east and she took it downward. A large, railed mezzanine stood over the great room below, blocking Alison's view. She took a moment to survey the scene. It took her no time to find the aberrant element across the open floor plan. Jesse Flores was standing before an open refrigerator, nursing a bottle of purple Pedialyte. He wore a powder blue tracksuit, college pin fixed to the lapel, and stood motionless, cradling the precious bottle in his arms. Alison wasted no time crossing the room with dire expediency. Five hard steps and four soft squishes and she was in the strike zone. She hammered a right hook into his stomach and he exploded, purple elixir spraying thoroughly onto the entirety of her personage. She caught a glimpse of shock and terror as he doubled over. She reached for the pin. He gave no fight, but the pin did. It wouldn't budge. She tightened her grip and pulled hard, tearing it from the tracksuit.

Something wasn't right. She glanced down at the pin, complete with torn fabric. It was a regular college pin. It was a set-up. She started toward the front door, reaching for her coms as she moved, but ran into a brick wall. It was Tyrannosaurus Ross. Sporting his best "I'm not mad, I'm disappointed" face, he grappled her forearm effortlessly in his colossal hand. And that was the end.

Relinquish control.

Wonder of wonders, miracle of miracles, a falling star came crashing down from the heavens that night to free Alison from her harrowing plight. But it wasn't a star. It was an All Star. A great, bloody, tumbling Converse All Star from the sky. It made a mountainous crack as it pummeled Danny Ross square in the back, blood softly misting the chic Danish furnishings that surrounded. Standing at the top of the mezzanine was Paige Hall, arms folded, a devilish grin on her playful features. Danny let go of Alison's arm out of shock and horror and disgust at the rude spectacle.

"Well, that's my cue," said Alison as she grabbed the crimson shoe and bolted for the entrance, leaving behind a mess fit for a Tarantino set. As she burst out the front door, she was greeted by Paige's deftly falling frame from a second story window. She was carrying Alison's other shoe. They gave each other a quick look and exited stage left.

"How did you find me?" Alison asked, out of breath and running the campus gauntlet in her bloody socks.

"Easy," said Paige. "I followed the blood."

Even in their dilapidated state, that earned a belly laugh.

The tone was somber as they entered the great hall of Leeds Theatre. McElroy, Butler, Dalton, and Pierce were standing, motionless and silent, their eyes fixed on the great Hamlet statue above. Both Rajas were gone. No alarms, no phone alerts, nothing. Alison looked to Ed Butler, their fearless leader, for guidance. But his lips were sealed. She looked to his Footman's pin. All that remained was the empty magnet at its base. He gave a little sigh and put his hands in his pockets. Looking around, the other assets seemed intact. Alison was about to ask what happened, when a voice came into the coms: both the public and private channels.

"What a night, guys!" It was Reed Baker. "It has been a long while since we Elephants were able to gain so much position in so little time. Alison, you didn't kill little Danny, did you?"

"I did not," she replied, mystified.

"That's too bad. I was kind of rooting for you in a wicked sort of way. Everybody likes to root for the underdog. But the underdogs don't really win, I don't think." The disheartened crew looked eager to retort, but no one said a word. Reed continued. "I suppose we'll see. Here are my notes, Alison. Do with them what you will. First, nobody's ever going to tell you his faction. Second, don't trust intelligence from opposing factions. Side note, when someone highlights a trap with a big, red marker, don't walk into it. Finally, and this one's important, never take a Raja without checking it for bugs." The line went dead there.

Silence permeated for a few moments before all eyes fell on Alison. They didn't seem judgmental or disappointed as she feared. Just, directionless. Finally, Paige broke the bubble.

"So, what do we do now?"

Alison shifted, a bloody sock squishing with a melancholy bleat as she did. "Find absolution, I guess." The Lord Chamberlain's Men nodded respectfully.

"I'll tell you one thing," Paige offered, her sprightly tone lightening the mood considerably. "The game's definitely afoot, now." She was about to close the file on that thought when her face lit up with a new energy. "Oh! That reminds me," she said, a wild grin emerging. "Here's your shoe, dear."

NINE

The dust finally seemed settled in Alison's mind as she entered Leeds for the first post-disaster meeting of The Lord Chamberlain's Men. The oversized theatre door creaked as she shouldered through, allowing a flood of hazy afternoon sunlight to momentarily illuminate the dark chamber. She was feeling calm again, albeit embarrassed about her leading role in depleting her faction's position to practically nil and generally ruining everything. At least the damage was done. It was time to move forward, broken pieces in tow, and figure out how to traverse the rough road ahead. Not exactly an easy task– considering she had just lost them a leader– but a clear one.

Perhaps that was the source of Alison's sense of resolution. Being directly responsible for the most dramatic one-night losses the faction had ever endured, she knew exactly where she stood. Which was most assuredly on the bench from here on. Maybe they'd let her play operator for a low-stakes mission after a month or two of cooldown. But she wasn't going to be in the field or planning any missions. And she certainly wasn't going to be calling audibles over the coms or making split-second decisions in any darkened Danish-modern frat houses.

And, while that was by far the best part, she knew it was time to let go.

Ten minutes early, and with the stalwart absolution of a Spartan phalanx captain whose shield had been mysteriously replaced with an oversized slice of toast, Alison sat cross-legged in a spot-lit easy chair and mulled her fate. She was, in fact, so lost in thought that she was visibly startled by a sudden realization that she had brought no music to her pity party. That needed immediate medical intervention, and she knew just the medicine. Earbuds already secured in place by deeply-rooted ritual, she conjured a phone and flicked about wildly until Miike Snow's dreamy pop synthesizers and pounding electric drums were floating in her brain.

Sometimes Alison felt a strong aversion to well-known and properly-appreciated music. As though her role in loving music was that of a rescue mom to beautiful and exotic shelter cats. She was reluctant to admit to enjoying songs that were popular or artists that had their fair share of attention. She also had a weird hang-up about enjoying any artist's top hit or most critically acclaimed track. For Miike Snow, however, she made an exception, because Genghis Khan was just an absolute treasure.

She was in fine spirits when a burst of errant sunlight ushered in a small crop of compatriots. She straightened her posture a little and folded her hands in her lap in an effort to appear ready to face the music. Alison's expectation of disappointed expressions from the group was vehemently denied in the entrance. In fact, they seemed downright jovial. Although Miike Snow was still do-do-do-ing a bouncy staccato interlude in her earbuds, she could see from the body language that her fellow assets were recounting the events of the previous sortie with tremendous mirth. Paige in particular was incited into bursts of nearly uncontrollable laughter by Teddy Dalton, who was making dramatic gestures of what could only be the vigorous spattering of blood. She then went on to mimic the sliding of a phone beneath a doorway and booking it a few steps in the other direction. Perhaps Alison had denied herself a little due credit after all.

The team shared a few bright hellos as they settled into their easy chairs. Sir Andy gave a courtly bow while extending a hand in Alison's direction, triggering a hearty applause and a handful of jaunty interjections. She smiled and gave a familiar little tug on the cord of her earbuds, who gently popped out of position and into her lap. She couldn't help but hide the confusion on her face. You simply don't get a ticker tape parade for screwing everything up. Nevertheless, she shifted to a pose of graceful acceptance, because that's show business. The party was however abruptly shuttered by the entrance of Control, whose air of sobriety immediately captured the attention of the assets. Now that was the irritated dad face Alison was looking for. Fussbudget Prime.

Peters made good theatrical use of the elongated silence as he slowly paced the gangway, the sound of brown, patent leather shoes echoing the proscenium in his wake. He traversed the steps to the high-crested stage and slid into his chair with a grave dose of pith and moment. The floor was all his; silent, eager eyes awaited his address. Slightly shocked at the gravity he'd apparently unwittingly induced, he finally spoke.

"Bally ho, dorks!" he rejoiced, and Alison's anxiety

melted as the snow under a chorus of swiftly-beaten armchairs.

With Ed Butler dead, there seemed to be an apparent vacuum of leadership. As the pleasantries and chair abuse died down, the assets began looking around nervously at each other, each hoping someone else would step up and facilitate the meeting. Control, who never wasted an opportunity to pontificate, took the reins immediately, to the company's general relief.

"Before we begin, we should take a moment to honor our fallen leader, Ed Butler, who gave his life so that we could continue on with this inane rubbish. Ed, wherever you are, probably in heaven or at the coin laundry, we will lift your banner and carry on. To Ed!"

And each asset leaned over the right arm of their easy chair, and simultaneously spit on the stage below. It was touching and it was weird. Control continued.

"And now, to business. We must select a new first-in-command. I should like to nominate Alison Ashe."

Alison jumped as though she'd just realized she'd been sitting on a bed of nails. "You what?"

"Do I have a second?"

"Hold on!"

"I second the motion," offered Teddy Dalton with gusto.

"What-"

"All in favor?"

"Hold, on, what-"

"Aye!" rang the entire chorus, unanimously, with the exception of an exasperated Alison Ashe.

"The actual-"

"All opposed?"

"Flumph."

Alison sat in shock, her jaw unfastened, her earbuds dangling like tiny pendulums. Paige took the opportunity to speak up.

"I don't think we're counting that. Please vote either 'aye' or 'nay' in the future, dear. In any case, the 'ayes' have it. Cheers, Alison."

When the inevitable circus faded, all eyes were on Alison. She gave a timid gulp, scratched her head for effect, and, forming a thoughtful pose, spoke. Her actual words were not nearly as humble nor eloquent as her posture suggested.

"So– um, why? I guess."

"Why what, dear?" said Paige, placing a cooling hand on Alison's knee.

"Why, um, me? I'm pretty sure I blew it."

"Oh, rather!" chimed Sir Andy.

"With due expediency," added Teddy Dalton, doing his best Jeeves.

"And–" Paige jumped in here, "it doesn't matter. You possess the proper qualities of a leader. Your mind paints in broad strokes; you never get tunnel-vision. You can delegate. You can trust and be trusted. You adapt to changing situations. You're bold, you're brave, you embrace gambits, and you take risks. I don't think any of The Lord Chamberlain's Men measure a leader by a checklist of wins and losses. Sometimes you do everything right and you still lose. I know for my money, I'd rather lose under your advisement than win under some watered-down Kroger-brand leader. You're a premium-label boo."

Control gave a small vocal cue to attain the floor, but took a moment to gather his thoughts before offering his piece. "It is perhaps your course of bold action that awarded us this unfavorable position. But now, we're here. In the proverbial soup, as it were. And from here, it is unequivocally clear that your particular flavor of bold action is our best shot at getting out."

"Undeniably," said Paige.

"Categorically," Andy McElroy roared.

"Indubitably," posited Teddy Dalton, a thoughtful gesture in tow.

"Yes," offered Brian Ward, speaking for the first time this meeting, and quite possibly ever.

The focus once again shifted to Alison Ashe. She took a moment to absorb the group's tragic application of logic, briefly floated the idea that they were experiencing some sort of mass-induced Stockholm Syndrome, and finally shifted expressions to indicate that she had accepted her fate.

"Alright," she said, a concoction of cynicism and sass leaking liberally from her tone, "but you asked for it."

***

Alison eyed the dimly lit corridor with scrutiny as Paige dragged her past its weird, old sconces. Everything was exceedingly dusty and the brick was the wrong color.

"Seriously, Paige. Where are you taking me?"

Paige, ignoring the question, thumbed the inner pocket of her black denim jacket and returned with a long, folding metal device. She dropped to a knee and began to guide its business end into a padlock barring a sizable wooden door, a look of intense concentration on her face.

"Is that a lockpick? Paige, why are you so cool?"

Paige offered a blithe smile over her shoulder when the padlock gave a satisfying click. Alison continued rambling, as though Paige had been answering her questions all along.

"Is this a crypt? Why are there weird passages beneath the theatre building? Is this where they bury dead faculty? Is this–" she gasped, "Was Bauer built on an ancient cemetery?"

Paige offered an expression she typically reserved for injured animals– or boys. The doorway led to a massive, black chamber with rounded walls. Chairs and music stands were strewn about, covered in thick dust.

"This," Paige finally revealed, "is the Orchestra Pit." She cut across at a bouncy pace, leading her companion to one last archway. Alison was caught off guard by the ominous majesty and struggled to keep up. Paige continued, "And this– is the rigging room. Our new secret spot."

The enormous underground hollow was filled with practical accouterments. Anchored ropes lined the eastern and western walls, tapering up through holes in the ceiling toward the lines above. Taught pulleys covered the northern face. A cavalcade of old par cans sat abandoned on errant shelving. A towering lighting board from the seventies basked under a blue work-light, its antique knobs and sliders crusted shut. In the center of the room was the piece de resistance: a colossal crash pad. Paige suddenly dashed towards it, planting a foot on a nearby black box and vaulting upwards, forming a single, lazy front tuck before landing on her back with a satisfying floof. Post-landing, she continued to slowly sink into its contours.

"What do you think?"

"Dang, Paige. It's perfect. How did you find this place?"

"I have my methods. Besides, I was motivated. We need a fresh start with pretty much everything now that we're basically compromised. A place to think, sans testosterone, seemed like a top priority."

"Seriously. Well, hot tamale, sugar bear. I don't know what I'd do without you."

"Me neither. Now gimme a boost."

Alison sidled onto the tall mat with the grace of a beached manatee and promptly folded her fingers and dropped into classic boost pose. Paige cleared what looked to be double her height, and deftly clasped a horizontal metal bar with both hands. Releasing a little latch to her right, she began to slowly float back down to earth, bringing a utility ladder with her and revealing a thin beam of light from the trap door above.

"Try the lever," she said, still hanging luxuriously and gesturing to an antiquated arm bar on the south wall. Alison hunkered over and gave it a tug. The ceiling exploded downward, revealing the magnificent ribbed vaults of Leeds, a tangled mass of lines and rigging, and a thousand lighting instruments above. Paige had released herself just in time to miss the wrath of the plummeting trap door and plopped smartly in the center of the mat.

After a moment of posing like she was auditioning for a Mattress Firm commercial, she folded her hands behind her head and beckoned Alison over with a nod. They took a minute to quietly contemplate the universe before Paige finally spoke.

"So how's all your actual real life going?"

"Oh. Jesus. I forgot about real life for a hot minute, there," Alison replied. "Well, I never gave Peters an answer about changing over to Theatre Tech. But I did start working as Fight Director, so it's possible he'll make an assumption and start flipping all the switches of my life for me. I'm kind of ready to be done with college, so I don't know about this MFA program nonsense."

"So what are you gonna do with your theatre BFA? Teach high school, or win a Tony for your one-woman rendition of Death of a Salesman?"

"Oh, dink right off, muffin. You're in the same boat."

"Um, no? I can tumble. I'll be in the chorus of Newsies or whatever else Kenny Ortega sneezes out next without batting an eyelash. And I'm not bragging or criticizing, Pooh Bear. I'm just going with the river. It seems like your river is fight directing."

"Ew," said Alison, objecting on principle to Paige's simple but undeniable reasoning.

"What?"

"Nothing. It's just– how can I spend weeks torturing myself over a decision and then you make the path sound so clear and obvious with a single sentence?"

Paige turned her head to face Alison and smiled sweetly. "Hm. Do you think maybe it's because you're a dumb trollop?"

Alison let out an indignant huff and took a swipe for Paige's left sneaker, a Vans Half-Cab. Swiftly removing the aforementioned footwear, she pitched it heartily through the trap door and into the theatre above. It sailed out of sight. All that remained was its memory, etched into Paige's expression of shock and betrayal. They laughed.

"Point taken," said Paige as the laughter subsided. "You know who *is* a dumb trollop? Casey Harrington." Alison let out a brief, monosyllabic laugh paired with her well-practiced expression of existential panic before Paige continued. "How the crunchberry are you going to teach that nautical nerf to fight?"

Alison sighed. "That seems like a problem that deserves critical reflection and thoughtful action."

"Mm, hm."

"So I think I'll just add it to the pile and sit on my hands until it blows up in my face."

"Mm, hm."

TEN

"Alison, what?" floated a muffled voice from beneath the second-story floorboards of the little powder blue house on West Court. The voice was right: she wasn't being a very good housemate at the moment. Normally, Alison's presence was minimal and unobtrusive. Absorbed in her work as a rule, she could typically be found curled tightly in her stupid egg chair, shielded from the universe by her Berydynamic over-ear headphones, quietly typing into oblivion. The chair was the most cliche college student thing she owned, which she hated, but she couldn't argue with the comfort and safety it offered as it perfectly matched the contours of her tall frame while quietly forgiving her terrible posture.

But slouch-and-study was a distant memory in this brave new world. Having accepted her fate as Hamlet's fight director, Alison had pushed all her furniture to the edges of her room to create a workspace to iron out complex exchanges and visualize patterns of movement. Her bed frame and mattress were propped against the far wall, blocking the window, leaving her almost nine square feet of hardwood to stomp, pounce, and pace about wildly. To the rest of the house, this translated to three or four loud thumps at a time, manifesting at random and unpredictable intervals, and which could be heard and felt in any room.

"Seriously, Aly, what on Earth?" Cara was standing in the doorframe now, a mint green facemask applied presumably to accentuate her Frankenstonian rage, and gesturing patently with a nail file. Alison had just completed a three-shot haymaker combination from the defender's point of reference, and it was dimes-to-doughnuts that Cara had just witnessed her getting beat up by an invisible combatant. And, to be fair, this must have been a particularly unsettling tableau for the type of person who just wanted to spend a quiet evening filing her nails and exfoliating.

To Alison, nothing had changed, really. She was, as ever, absorbed in her work. The work itself had changed but *that's life, am I right?* She attempted this line of reasoning with Cara, but in typical Alison fashion, skipped a few steps.

"Yeah. So, I'm just– working out a fight for Act V, Scene II and– you know what? It's pretty much the same as before because I'm doing the same thing, but it's just a different *thing* that I'm doing."

Cara did not have the tools to respond to this. She slowly scanned the room, its furniture strewn wildly. This, compounded with Alison's out-of-breath rambling, and the colossal beating she had apparently just taken from a ghost, was too much. She swallowed, slowly lowered the nail file, and left.

The message, however, was clear to Alison. She was taking on too much, and some of it was spilling out.

***

There were perks, however, to Alison's decision to step up to the plate. This was a leadership role. That meant front-page billing in the playbill, the final decision on integral elements of the play, and a seat at the top table for design and production meetings. If Alison felt the "Who's there?" between Bernardo and Francisco in Act I implied a fight, she had the power to arrange a bare-knuckle boxing match right there in the lobby of Elsinore Castle. She was also expected to lead weekly conditioning workouts and stage combat rehearsals for any actors with fighting roles. Her name was now listed as Student/ Faculty in the Bauer directory, an accolade that came with a small stipend and an office of her choosing, in which she was required to hold regular office hours. Being in the BFA Acting program always felt diminutive to Alison– as though she were always fighting for her life, ever on the precipice of losing her in-company status if she couldn't pony up the goods. This was different. BFA Tech made her feel like a boss. She found immediate preference for navigating this new world, even if the extra responsibilities sometimes made her feel like a leaky levee.

These items were amongst Alison's first quiet contemplations made from her first office at her first sitting of office hours– though the term office need be applied very loosely to the quirky rehearsal hall/storage room in the basement of Lyman Hall she had selected for her own. The large, rectangular room was equipped with the painted hardwood flooring of a black box theatre, and enough room to navigate complex blocking. However, at some point, the Properties Department must have called dibs on this particular space for their storage overflow, as its walls were lined with shelving that housed a menagerie of the most peculiar implements. Old books, candelabras, musical instruments, and a great assortment of liquor bottles gave the room the ambiance of a posh Victorian study. Alison had pushed a couple of black-boxes into a corner near a drink globe (currently housing her water bottle) to form a makeshift nook– one that would vaguely resemble a desk if she weren't seated on the floor, knees curled to her chest, atop an ornate orange throw pillow. She was just writing down the phrase "Leaky Levee" in a notebook, under a list entitled "Nicknames for Paige," when the door opened, revealing the scurvy-ridden scallywag Casey Harrington.

"If it isn't the Dread Pirate Casey," she found herself saying, suddenly wishing for a chair. You can banter from a chair. It's harder to banter on a throw pillow.

"Aly, hey!" he said, her quip having flown about as high above his head as an admiral's pennant, delicately draped from the mizzen mast. "I was just– is this your office?"

"Yes, Casey," she replied. "Is that what you're looking for, or are you lost?" Apparently, she was too tired to force any further unregistered sea puns, but still had enough feudal spirit to compare him to a lost child.

"Yeah, the schedule said this was your office hours."

"The schedule was correct."

"Oh, okay, tight," he offered, an infuriating pause between each hand-picked utterance.

"Yes, Casey, it's very tight," she affirmed. And, after an excruciatingly prolonged silence, threw in a slightly frustrated "What do you want?"

"Right, yeah. So, I'm Hamlet, and you're the fight director."

"Your memory is spotless."

"Thanks. So, I was hoping, if I come in for your office hours, that you could teach me how to do stage combat. Just the basics, you know?"

"Casey. Haven't you taken Stage Combat I and II?"

"I've been putting it off. It seemed like a whole thing, you know?"

Alison did not know. She always took prerequisite courses as soon as they were available, so she could qualify for as many roles as possible. Casey's *devil may care* attitude was at very least unthinkable, if not impossible to square in this program. But somehow it didn't matter. Either nobody bothered to ask him, or he was granted some sort of exception. That, or he pulled some sort of New England affluence judo with his parents' annual gifts to the college. This thought would have made Alison's blood boil, except, it was already boiling on something else. When auditioning for the role of Hamlet, she had been asked, explicitly and twice, whether or not she had completed Stage Combat II, which was required for the role. She took a breath to gain her composure and tried to swallow her hellfire, because this had just evolved into a full blown crisis.

"Casey! This is a disaster for you!"

But as soon as she said it, she realized: this was a disaster for her. Casey Harrington's K-Mart brand telenovela acting was his own. But his fighting would reflect on her. It could even put people in danger if his body control was anything like his control of the English language. This was honestly what riled Alison up the most about gender inequity. If the patriarchy was composed of a convocation of shrewd, thoughtful men and she was out-competed, fine. But the men she witnessed getting the edge at Bauer were all part of an inane chorus line of infantile, flaxen potatoes. And now she either had to tie Casey's shoes for him or shoulder the blame for his ineptitude. Even so, she wasn't sure it could be pulled off.

"It took me a semester of training to get the basics," she continued. "And I'm good."

"I could be good," he retorted.

"You're wearing boat shoes and chinos!" She took a moment to smirk at her comment. He looked mildly offended.

"Hey, now. I'll have you know that deck shoes are the ultimate in comfort and versatility. In my time on the sailing team–"

"Oh, honey," she cut him off with a sweet, mothering tone. "No." That would have been enough for her, but he looked less than convinced. "Here, I'll show you. Square off." He slid his left foot backward, bent his knees slightly, and lifted his fists, knuckles out, like he was trying out for the Peaky Blinders. She resisted the urge to say "Jesus Christ" and instructed him to throw a right hook.

"I don't want to hurt you," he said, in all seriousness. If Paige were in the room, she would have snorted. Alison simply blinked.

"I'll be okay," she said, dropping into her fighting stance. "Go ahead."

He took a step forward and started shifting his weight for the punch. Alison deftly tucked her head under the aperture of the blow in a fluid motion, lunging forward toward Casey and stepping on his foot. She placed a hand on his solar plexus and gave the slightest push, still leaning securely on his loafer. His equilibrium already thrown off, he lost his back footing, and, sans any traction from the slick-soled boat shoe, slid back into the splits.

"Oh, wow," he said, taking stock of the situation. A realization hit his face, which Alison prayed to wise Athena was more along the lines of "This is going to be harder than I thought" and less akin to the sort of "I wonder if Taco Bell still has those tacos with the Doritos cheese dust" sort of thoughts that must be swimming in his head so often. She helped him to his feet and gave him a moment to gather his composure. He locked eyes with her and took the sort of breath you take when you have something to say that holds a modicum of gravity. Alison crossed her mind's fingers in hopes that this wasn't a cheese dust thought.

"You're worried that I'm not going to work hard," he said, clearly more socially aware than she had given him credit for.

"Yes," she said, simply.

"Normally, I only work as hard as I have to. Maybe that comes off as lazy."

"Yes," she repeated. If he was going to just hand her low-hanging fruit, she was going to take it.

"But this is a wicked wedge, and I don't think there's any other path."

It occurred to Alison that this was a recurring impasse in her life: whether or not to trust a guy to do as he says. It double-sucked because:

1. She usually got burned, and
2. She believed in the goodness of humankind,

whatever that meant.

"Okay, Casey," she said after another elongated inner-diatribe. "We'll– get you caught up. I'll show you a few things today that you can do in your chinos. Next week, show up in normal-person athletic wear." She paused a moment, a mildly acerbic thought arising in the wake of her mildly embittered recollection that some people face a lot more wicked wedges than others, and continued. "Actually, you should buy some yoga pants."

***

First off, she was going the wrong way.

Alison still had Directing II to get to before she could hang her hat for the day. But her head was full of static and the sky had taken on that dark kind of overcast that promised rain even when it was cold enough to snow. She liked the cold well enough. It enabled her to wear her military jacket with the faux-fur-lined hood– the one Paige affectionately called her "Ranger Jacket." But crisp, cold air and a cozy coat couldn't quell the gloom that lined Alison's leaden heart after signing up for a course of regular and repeated interactions with Admiral Dirtbag. And, without the benefit of clear thought, she autopiloted home with a heavy stride and a well-worn Father John Misty record to take the edge off. Nancy From Now On was just the medicine she needed as she took in a long breath and considered what fresh horrors awaited her from the dark corners of her day planner.

Alison did not know this yet, but her temper had become a precariously-wavering Jenga tower whose structurally-essential center bricks had been delicately relocated by a full course load, newfound directorial responsibilities, an all-consuming game that seemed more vivid than real life, and an infinitely-frustrating salty sea bass who will not be named. An only child and a serial avoider of conflict, Alison had little practice getting in touch with her emotions. Her fuse needed to be lit before she could see she even had one. And, it so happened that on this pithy pity-walk, while her mind buzzed like a can of bees, Alison caught a glimpse of the straw that made the camel mad.

It was a brown duffel coat.

With a spring in her step and a "Not today, Satan" in her heart, she took off towards the little turd. He had been tucked away, almost out of sight behind a Baroque outcropping protruding from the exterior of Sharpe House. But Alison was now finely-tuned to the visage of brown duffel coats and the mysterious movements of those within. He took a moment to register what he was seeing as Alison bounded in his direction, fiery-eyed, a Pamplonan bull who had just caught sight of a corn-fed American tourist in red stretch pants. He hoisted himself over the low wall guarding the building and tried to cut the corner towards Angell Street. But Alison was in no mood, and exploded right through the hedgerow that blocked the interim path. He let out a stifled cry as she smashed into him, the mass of bodies tumbling into the dry, dead grass underfoot.

Alison kipped to her feet with stunning dexterity. Her mark started shifting to rise as well, but she stopped him with a raised index finger.

She had a lot to say, but, mind muddled, all she could

muster was an exasperated "What." On reflection, it got the point across.

"Yeah, I– guess now is as good a time as any that we meet officially," he said, out of breath. "You can call me– X."

Alison bent down, placing her hands on her knees and bringing her face a little closer to his. "I am not calling you that. Show me your ID and unlock your phone for me or I will kill you, and then kick you in the breakfast nook."

The soft poetry appeared to move him, and he complied accordingly.

"Nick Rodgers," she said absently as she scrolled through his email. A slew of messages from the College of Psychology verified beyond a reasonable doubt that he was Chariot. She tossed the phone back to him. "What do you do for Chariot, Nick Rodgers?"

"I'm an intelligence broker. I trade what I know to the highest bidder. That is, assets that might be in possession of information we need. You've been on our list of potential clients for a few months. We used to have a contact in Footmen. Tony Keane. We worked on a mission together before he–"

"Call him. Put it on speaker."

Nick did as he was told. Tony's voice registered on the line, a cheery "Nick, how the heck are you?" Satisfied, Alison reached in and ended the call.

She took a beat before returning her gaze back to the humiliated mass that remained of Nick Rodgers. "Why didn't you just talk to me, instead of shadowing me like a psycho?"

"I was afraid you'd kick me in the breakfast nook."

"Fair point. Why should I trade intel with you?"

"Because we want the same thing."
"And what's that?"
"For Elephant to lose."

ELEVEN

"Mom, what?"

Alison's voice was agitated as she tucked her phone between her ear and her shoulder. A small, green spiral notebook, rife with furious markings, occupied her left armpit as she grappled with an uncooperative ballpoint pen, the stuck zipper on her open backpack, and now her phone, whose insidiously tangled earbud cable had entered the negotiation as well. The driver of a white Fiat had now come to a complete stop, patiently accepting Alison's temporary occupation of Prospect Street, under the assumption that the frustrated juggling act– perhaps some sort of performance art– would eventually subside and life would return to normal. It would, for him. Alison, however, was vaguely aware that her holistic and interdisciplinary tailspin was still in its early stages. She had two papers due, a circus of spies looking to her for guidance in a game she didn't fully understand, Casey Harrington was shaping up to have two left peg-legs, and her mother was in real danger of literally dying of capitalism.

It was this last point that, in fact, pushed her over the edge of irritation. She was no stranger to a mid-intersection inventory reconfiguration. Had the Fiat honked, she would have neither blushed nor been moved towards the palms-down fast walking prevalent in like circumstances. But a call from Irene Ashe, whose cable news binging had recently inspired her to block caller ID for some paranoid reason Alison was far too tired to hear, was too rich for today's palate. While she truly loved and respected her mother, some unholy combination of Facebook, Costco, and 24-hour news had begun to cultivate attitudes and behaviors that caused Alison to experience a visceral, physical reaction that could previously only be set into motion by the incoherent ramblings of dreary, suburbanites with anti-vax email signatures. Irene wasn't spouting keto or chemtrail nonsense, but something about the time and the tone made every diatribe sound the same these days. And as such, when the phone started buzzing and Alison saw "Unknown Caller" flash onto the display, she very decidedly couldn't even.

A good old fashioned "Mom, what?" would have indeed been the perfect opening line to set the tone for a short conversation as Alison traversed the Quad in search of a quiet corner for study and the anxious consumption of lukewarm tuna salad. She was, however, firmly taken aback to hear a male voice manifest on the line instead.

"Alison, hello," crooned Reed Baker, smooth as Fred Astaire, and completely unfazed by the abrupt and erroneous salutation. His cool demeanor was an absolute air raid on Alison's composure, and she responded accordingly.

"What in Jiminy's sake do you want? Are you going to trick me into giving you my Netflix password? Are you going to make me buy a timeshare? Or maybe I can just give you my social security number."

"Actually, this is a social call."

"Are you an actual moron?" snapped Alison, heat rising in her voice. "Wait. Did you have a traumatic brain injury? That's actually at the top of my list of reasons that you could possibly want a social call."

"Well, I–"

"Hold, on, hold on. Hang on a sec. No, I get it. You're calling to schedule a hot date, aren't you? A moonlit walk on the veranda whilst we share a snifter of Napoleon's private cognac reserve. I'm sure it's aged nicely over the last two hundred years in oak casks sealed in your family's catacombs with beeswax and cedar bungs."

"So, what I'd like to–"

"Do you think I'm your quirky little dream girl? That I've just been sitting around waiting for your call beside my vintage typewriter collection? Deciding which hand-made polka-dotted dress to wear when you finally decide to give me your varsity pin?"

Reed politely waited a beat, in case there was more.

"No," he assured her. "I'm not seeking a star-crossed romance. More of a– friendship– I suppose." He paused for any possible quips this might have elicited. When the line remained silent, he continued. "You may have guessed that engineers can be a little dry, and a little serious. The Elephants this year are exceptionally serious. But the game is supposed to be fun. It occurred to me that the only times I've had fun this season involved interacting with you. I have a lot of– professional respect– for you. I like the way you play the game, and

I like the way you express yourself. I thought maybe we could– compartmentalize. And talk sometimes."

"You're not my friend, Reed. You're my– my nemesis."

"Okay, now that's something I can live with. A nemesis isn't just an enemy. It's a special kind of relationship. It involves respect and reverence. You keep a nemesis in your thoughts. You consider their perspectives. You leave your finger on the chess piece while you study their expression, looking for tells. Alison, I would be honored to be your nemesis."

Alison laughed. Her mouth was full of tuna. Somehow, she'd been magically transported to a little secluded bench in the gardens under Carrie Tower, and was stress-eating her sandwich. Also magically, she had a colossal smile on her face and was experiencing some sort of distant emotion. *Joy?* she thought. *Is this joy? Why? I know, definitively, that I actively hate this man. Do I– enjoy– hating him? What is wrong with me?*

"Hum" was the best she could muster, however, for the moment. Reed waited until he was sure that was all.

"I realize it's a lot," he said. "I just– I don't know why we can't appreciate the other side. I've been made aware of the bloody shoe and the William Shatner decoy play. I need you to know that that's the funniest thing that's ever happened in this game."

Alison let go of a small fragment of the massive chip on her shoulder at that, and threw in a good belly laugh for good measure. It felt somehow cathartic to be appreciated by her rival. Maybe it was okay to share some of the excitement of the game with the other factions. It was only a game, after all, though Alison would be hard pressed to find an asset who would admit it.

"Okay, but like, did you see the room? When I hit Flores with that gut punch, he popped like a pinata. I got sprayed so thoroughly with purple Pedialyte I could have got a permanent job at Nickelodeon."

Reed liked the image. "Yeah, the whole thing was a very dark episode of Double Dare. How did you get so bloodied in the first place?"

"Caught my ankle on the SAE fencing when I popped over."

"The pikes!"

"The pikes," Alison confirmed. "But if I hadn't been sliced open, I wouldn't have had a suitable snack to appease the mighty Spork."

"Jesus, Alison. I forgot about that dog! You really insist on doing everything the hard way."

Alison considered. "As opposed to what? Walking into your trap through the front door?"

Reed laughed again as the energy of the call became more friendly. "I just wish I could have seen your face when you tore Jesse's pin off of his tracksuit."

"Oh, I can help you with that, Reed," said Alison in a caustic-but-cheery tone. "It was my annoyed face. The one I make when I'm doing business with you. It's the face I show you more than any other. Statistically, it's my default face, as far as you're concerned."

"Okay," retorted Reed. "Then it also had a little smirk hiding in the wings."

Alison gasped facetiously. "Reed Baker. Are you implying that I enjoy despising you?" He was. She did.

"Not my words. But if you did, I'd be a suitable candidate for nemesis."

Alison let out an exasperated sigh, to her own chagrin.

He was right. What she needed right now was a nemesis. And Reed, despite his diabolical tactics and his stupid, freckled, cute, stupid face, was it. God knows Casey Harrington wouldn't be able to keep up with her. That little nerf couldn't find a quip if it were on the Post-It with all his passwords. "Fine, you can be my nemesis. But give me your word that you won't use this line to sabotage, double-cross, or betray me in any way."

"You have my word, Alison."

"A lot of good that's worth," she countered, wrapping up the business at hand before sharply changing tone. "Okay, bye mom. Feel better. I love you!"

And she hung up the phone.

What Reed Baker did not understand, for he had not the tools, was that Paige Hall had in that moment rounded the corner, spotted Alison, and plopped down in the seat across from her. Alison's composure was severely compromised by this turn of events, and the ratio of tuna consumed versus tuna on her lap was becoming an indicator. She tried to play it cool.

"What's up, my little drama llama?"

"More like trauma llama these days," said Paige. "This semester is literally killing me."

"Right?"

"I'm feeling burnout, Alison. I'm memorizing lines in all my free time. Period Styles is a stupid waste of a class. I have a paper due on pumpkin pants."

"Okay, woah now. Stop right there," said Alison, a look of feigned concern on her face. "Do you want to go to Oleander's right now and study pumpkin pants over pumpkin lattes?"

"That is exactly correct."

Alison was feeling some relief that Paige hadn't overheard her conversation with Reed, but the whole moment was rewritten by the sudden piggy-back ride she was giving her small-framed friend. She had sort of slithered up there when Alison wasn't looking.

"Onward, drama llama! Oh, how's mama?" said Paige, clicking her heels where the spurs would be.

"Oh, fine."

***

"And you're certain you can't tell us your source for this intel?" Teddy Dalton offered, a stark beam of light from the garden windows catching the corners of his face as he leaned in.

Andrews Commons was an open meeting place, a high-ceilinged lounge great for studying and catching up. Unlike much of the drab, red brick pomp-and-circumstance of Bauer's central building cluster, the outskirts tended to be more modern. The massive glass orange-slice windows dropped a splash of morning light on the midcentury leaf chairs and bright red couches that spread endlessly across the hall. Little shops and coffee stands dotted the perimeter. A lot of foot traffic moved in and out of the commons, and there was always a dull din of conversation. Alison had arrived early to gather her thoughts. She had been a little indecisive on today's playlist, flipping back and forth between Ben Harper and Neko Case, and, uncharacteristically departing from tracks before their completion. She had just decided on House Fire by Someone Still Loves You, Boris Yeltsin, when Teddy popped into the frame.

"Respectfully," Alison replied, "I will be unable to answer that quandary until three minutes and nineteen seconds have elapsed with my head on this table."

Palms up, he bally-hoed her the space she needed, gesturing apologetically as he tucked himself out of the way. Alison did as she promised, hitting play on her phone and dipping into a deeply personal space. Broom was a comfort album for her, and, while she most appreciated its opus track in its natural habitat, she was willing to expedite in an emergency. The soft arpeggios floated sweetly over the lo-fi drums, diffusing a wave of calm outward from Alison's slow, deliberate breath. When the verse moved into the riffy pre-chorus, she made a decisive fist. There must have been a mile between those two moments.

When Alison emerged from her stasis, she found herself sharing the table with Dalton, McElroy, Ward, and Hall. She started in.

"No, the source can't be revealed. Neither the intel nor the source can be trusted. And, I gave real intelligence in exchange."

The group exchanged glances, but no sound of disapproval was emitted. Alison was calling the shots. If she had a strong feeling about something, they were usually happy to trust it. Surprisingly, nobody asked what she gave up in exchange for the lead. She took a moment to appreciate that fact, because she really didn't want to say. Alison waited a beat for questions and continued.

"We're going after the Rock."

Alison had been sure that four individuals speaking in unison was a feat reserved for sitcoms and cartoons, and found herself slightly taken aback by the volley that followed– albeit not entirely surprised by the content. They all simply said "No."

"Okay, but hear me out: yes," she responded, a sly smile pushing through.

Rockefeller Library was home to the Chariot Raja, and was by far the trickiest hit to pull off in Chaturanga for a number of reasons. It was open and populated at all hours of the day and night. One of the quintessential locations on campus, it was a hot spot for tours, study, meetups, and hangouts. It was the home of many of Bauer's rare books and relics, including a museum's worth of priceless fine art. This meant not only Chaturanga security, but real, actual security. This year, the Department of Psychology was borrowing a collection of dadaist pieces which were proudly displayed in the Altman Gallery. Their Raja shared a pedestal with Duchamp's Fountain. Taking it would be an actual heist, and could put an asset in actual prison.

After the pregnant silence, Dalton spoke first. "Nobody actually goes after the Chariot Raja. We pick off their assets until they fizzle or sell out another faction."

"That's us," chimed Paige. "We're the faction they're selling out. If we fail, we're topsoil, and if we succeed, we've got a target on our backs."

"Exactly," returned Alison.

"Exactly what?" Andy McElroy fired back. "We want to draw fire?"

The no's were more spread out than the last round, but they all came through. Teddy Dalton spoke first.

"We can't win a numbers war. We don't have the numbers. No faction has ever won outside of a Raja strategy."

"Yet," said Alison in a hopeful tone. "Elephant has three Rajas. We need to shake things up. Spread the pieces around the board a little."

"What do you have in mind?" replied Brian Ward. The table took another beat because, not only was he actually speaking, but it looked like Alison was somehow winning him over.

"Glad you asked, Brian. When we have the Raja–"

"If we can get it at all," Dalton interrupted. Alison was unfazed.

"When we have the Raja, we don't come home."

Dalton was getting heated. "The rules state that we have to display the acquired objective at our operations base."

Alison smiled. "Well, we don't come straight home. We take the long way. And take a little pit stop at Watson."

After a pause to process the sheer shock of what she was saying, the energy changed. Ward was the first to laugh.

When the air cleared, Paige spoke. "Okay, let me make sure I smell what the Rock is cooking. You're proposing that we somehow successfully steal the Chariot Raja, and then give it to the Cavalry."

"Yes."

"And then– what? Just sit back and watch the bloodbath between the other three factions?"

Alison folded her fingers together, resting her chin on their soft nest. "Yes."

And there was only one thing to say to that.

"Spicy."

TWELVE

The stale air in Alison's office smelled exactly like her grandmother's attic: dust, old furniture, and a certain tiredness that she could only detect in forgotten places. If her secret theory was correct, that discarded souls were collected and stored in doilies, then this room had a fine vintage collection of spectral funk. There weren't a lot of buildings on campus that still made use of incandescent light, and the soft, singular bulbs of Props Storage Room B let off a tiny note of amber that made the place feel otherworldly and special. The circulation wasn't great, but it was enough to send motes of dust dancing upward towards the warm light. The strange decor and secluded nature of the space gave Alison some comfort and security, which she had desperately needed with all she had on her plate. The old world tapestries and Greek busts contrasted sharply against transistor radios and bakelite kitchen sets. It was a hodgepodge of forgotten everything, and it was exactly the sort of place that Alison could slow down, take a breath, and figure out how she would get through the week.

It was also where she beat up rich boys. Well, only one, currently, and it was by his own request. But Casey Harrington should count as two. At least one for all the stupid anchors, and another entire person's worth of undue confidence. If he actually had a boat, it would be called The Confidently Wrong. Whatever the final tally, Casey tested Alison's patience with a significantly higher potable strength than the average New England trust fund baby, which was a lot to begin with.

There was one item with regard to himself that he underestimated, however: his physical strength. As he practiced his exchanges in rehearsal and in private lessons, he routinely came in way too hot. This was a problem for grapples, and this was especially a problem for swings. Even his knaps, where he was to mimic the sound of a blow, were coming through too hard, as evidenced by the sizable bruises he'd been giving himself on his forearm and thighs. And, as much as Alison treasured the fact that he was beating himself up, she had to slow him down, or someone (else) was going to get seriously hurt. This thought had been floating somewhere near the top of Alison's mind when he came at her in a lesson at the tail end of a three hit combination with enough momentum to make an entrance in the tradition of the Kool Aid man. The third strike, a haymaker, was supposed to be blocked, but she could tell it was going sour while telegraphing the blow and press-rolled instead. The momentum of Casey's wild swing sent him hurtling towards the empty space where Alison once was, and the power of the strike was a lot more than he was planning. He stumbled forward as the centripetal motion twisted his torso sideways, causing his knee to buckle hard. When he bit the dust, he rolled into a suit of armor, which crumpled on impact.

"Casey!" Alison exclaimed, but waited to say more. If he

was injured, this would be a rather different conversation, and admonishment wouldn't be of much help. He got up and dusted himself off, looking unscathed enough.

"Lost my footing a little, there. I thought there was a block on the haymaker."

"Casey!" she repeated. "You would have broken my arm! You're going way too hard. Why?"

He thought about this for a moment, an unusual feat for the surefire swabby. But he took Alison seriously, and was willing to be introspective for her sake, even if the software was a bit of a heavy load for the little Commodore 64 he had spinning around in his skull. "I guess I don't know my own strength," he finally offered.

"Well, you have to do better, Harrington. There's no room for error in this. If you did that on stage, you would have hurt someone. Period. Eighty percent power and speed. No more, okay?"

"Jesus," he returned. "You're right. I am so sorry. I never even thought about that. You know, like my weight, and my strength, and like, um, energy." He was scraping together a fairly sparse collection of remnants from high school physics, but Alison appreciated the effort.

Alison changed her tone a little. "Can I ask you something, Casey?"

"Yeah, of course."

Alison took a moment to consider how she might word this. She decided to just go for it. "Has anyone ever asked you to consider how your circumstances affect the way you interact with the rest of the world?"

He gave it some thought and landed on "Honestly, no."

"Okay, well, let's give it a shot, eh? Think about some of your advantages."

He looked lost. "Like, you mean, money?"

"Yeah. That's an advantage. Does having money influence how you see others?"

"Yes."

"It does? Tell me about that."

He spoke right away. "Well, last year my dad got me LASIK, and now I can see others really well."

Alison laughed, then made quick eye contact to make sure that was actually a joke. "You never struck me as a pun guy."

"Most of my jokes are actually by accident, if you can believe that."

She could.

Casey continued. "But no, I understand what you're saying. How does that apply to this situation?"

Alison pondered this. "Let's focus on your physical strength for a moment."

"Okay, but, like, I would never hurt anybody."

Alison stopped herself from reacting. This was actually starting to look productive. She continued. "Yeah, but you could. And that affects others. Like women, for example. If a woman is walking across campus at night, and you're going the same direction, but twenty feet behind her, she's going to feel uncomfortable. Every woman I know has a story about being followed by some creep. And a lot worse than that."

He processed. "Okay. So, if I'm not a creep, that's something, right?"

"Yes," Alison replied. "That's the bare minimum."

"But what else can I–"

Alison raised her eyebrow, but didn't interject. This was

his moment to figure it out. She waited, hoping the load wouldn't blow out his circuits.

He gave it a try. "Wait. You already answered that. I can– think about my situation in the context of like, the bigger situation."

Alison gave affirmative finger guns. "Not too shabby, Casey. Let's take a five and try the combination again. Tommy and Paige are coming in at two, and then we can run it with them in the frame. Maybe you can, like, not hurt them."

Casey took a cathartic breath. "Yeah, that sounds tight. Thank you, Aly. You may not believe this, but nobody has ever talked about that stuff with me."

"Oh, I believe it, Case."

***

Suzie Garcia gave Alison an exasperated and incredulous look as the soft, blue mood lighting brushed cool on the corner table at Mother of Runes, a chic but clandestine bar tucked away on Bath Street. Rosewood and succulents were illuminated by drop fixtures that splashed ambiance on old brick and polished concrete floors. Alison looked back at Suzie over two Boulevardiers in rocks glasses with burnt oranges as garnishes. The normally bright red Campari looked a drab purple in the low light, though flashes of crimson seeped through in the flicker of candles. Suzie broke the silence.

"You know my style, Alison. I have a dialectic. I'm an oil painter. Baroque. Bloom lighting. I can't just start doing a bunch of Yoko Ono business. And you want me to get on this– what– performance art?"

Alison laughed a little. She had never thought she'd be anywhere near the avant garde side of the coin either. "More of an– installation."

"Oh, god, Aly. That's even worse."

"How is it worse?"

"Okay, not worse, but like, another kind of equally bad."

Alison chewed on the situation. She knew she needed the smoke and mirrors treatment to make Altman Gallery even remotely approachable, and that meant foot traffic. Suzie, who had served as Alison's babysitter in her latchkey preteen years, was now an accomplished artist in the MFA Studio Art program. She was finishing her second year and was still shopping around for a venue for her spring series. She came out with a bang the previous year with an Artemisia study that had sparked conversation about covert feminism in the Renaissance. The follow-up would need to hold up to that standard, and Alison hoped that scoring a show in the Rockefeller could be just the carrot to get Suzie to overrun the place with a charcuterie of pretentious art nerds. *Come to think of it, charcuterie sounds good.* She decided she'd get some of that, too.

"How'd you even score the Altman, Al?"

Alison sipped her drink. It was more bitter and herby than she was expecting, but it finished sweet. "I started a club. Clubs on campus can make facilities requests for events. I just put our little gala on the little form and sent it in. Got an email twenty four hours later."

"What club? Don't you need a faculty adviser to start a club?"

Alison put on her cool face. At least, she thought it was cool. Confidence with a little smirk. "I just put the form on Peters's desk. He signed it without thinking. I doubt he even read it. I've been dropping a lot of paperwork on him lately for my department change and student-faculty designation. The club is called 'Exploring Boundaries at Bauer College.'"

"Hm. That easy." Suzie took a meditative sip and considered. "It's weird, right? A lot of these barriers to prestige are just– imaginary. Apparently, you can just fill out a form and do whatever you want."

Alison folded her fingers. She didn't care much for prestige, but decided not to speak on that as it was a necessary currency in Suzie's corner of the art world. Like it or not, she had some to bargain with. She gave Suzie some space to consider, hoping access to the Altman would be enough to push the poor woman towards the night of utter atrocities she had planned. She took a moment to admire the song that had just snuck in with the lights in the shared goal of making everyone in the bar feel super cool. It was working, but to be fair, Kasabian was just plain cheating on that metric.

This particular track, Club Foot, just bled cool. The synths pounded square waves over buzzy guitars and driving, electronic kicks. The hooky background vocals and fast four-four beat lulled Alison into a waking trance. Her heart rate accelerated, syncing up with the heavy drums and wild lyrical outbursts. She glanced down, catching her ring finger tapping in fours to the driving, electrical storm of rock and roll plasma.

Alison took a speaking breath, but didn't speak. She took the pause in conversation as an opportunity to consider her position. If her plan was going to have any chance of working, she'd need a canvas of confusion sufficient to create plausible deniability, which meant that Altman Gallery needed to be packed. Suzie was the only artist on campus capable of bringing in the foot traffic she needed. The problem of course was that she wasn't a fit for a gallery full of dadaists and challenges to traditional forms. She'd need some finessing to hang her work next to blank canvases and a urinal. The untied thread lingered in Alison's mind. Perhaps there was a way to work it to her advantage.

She knew she'd have to answer some questions about this wild ride, and she was still figuring out the details of how to sound "not crazy." It was a tall order, and she decided ultimately that she'd settle for "not entirely crazy."

"So, why me?" Suzie finally asked. "It's not like I'm exploring any boundaries. My style is like four hundred years old."

Alison hadn't exactly thought about this, but her head was full of Kasabian-related adrenaline and she found herself able to roll with it. "That's the thing, Suze! The contrast! We're putting your series in the same room with Duchamp and Maciunas and all the weirdos. I mean– we're always looking at that stuff in a vacuum. We never get to scrutinize it against the backdrop of like– art art."

Suzie absorbed that thought. "So, you want to do an avant garde show that undermines itself?"

"You could say it's the ultimate expression of avant garde."

Suzie sighed. "You see, this is why I hate this stuff. It's always so meta. This piece is asking questions about the nature of art and that piece wants us to examine the emptiness of humanity through the perspective of a cat by looking at a mirror through a spool of white yarn. And, like, at some point you're just too tired to argue."

Alison laughed, giving her cocktail another pull as she considered. The comment, and probably the bourbon, shook loose a little spark in her, and she decided to pivot slightly.

"Suzie. If you could paint a series that would be hung in the same room as Duchamp's readymades, what would it be?"

"Oh, I don't know. Probably oil masterwork depictions of his pieces. A urinal and a bike wheel and whatever, but, in Renaissance perfection. Show how much actual work goes into actual art."

Alison took another sip and placed her drink down on the table like a chess piece revealing a devastating pin. She knew it was over. "So, if you could do that, would you?"

"Come on, Alison, I–"

Alison waited. No need to say anything more. Suzie was dead to rights, and it was her own idea that did her in. It was a worthy endeavor, and a whopper of an opportunity. And it was the perfect next step for her graduate career. On top of that Suzie was the only one who could pull it off. Alison settled in to enjoy the music and her drink and the beautiful bar while Suzie examined the pieces on the board one last time. There was no fighting it. It was checkmate. Suzie let out a sigh and buried her head in her hands. Alison had earned it, fair and square. She gave her answer.

"I hate you. I'll do it."

THIRTEEN

"That's gonna be a hard maybe for me, Paige."

"Uh uh. Nope. Not gonna fly, babe." Paige gave Alison a skeptical but familiar look. "We're getting you out of your comfort zone."

Alison let out an overblown sigh, half joking, half deadly. "A party?"

"A gathering. It's nothing. Jenny and Jon are just off campus. They're setting up a projector in their backyard and a few people are going to come over and watch Pee Wee's Big Adventure." Alison signaled to speak, but Paige cut her off. "You can drink bubble water with a little lime in it. Nobody cares what you drink. And I'll sweeten the pot with chicken tendies if you can't bring yourself to eat grown up food."

Alison did an encore performance of her sigh, for the fans. "Paige! Don't bring chicken tendies into this. Honey mustard?"

"It can be arranged. I know a guy."

Alison huffed again, while the huffing was good. "It actually sounds really nice. I want to go, but my internal clock on visiting mom is past due. I haven't even heard from her in two weeks. I'm worried about her."

"You can't call?"

"No, I need to drop in. If she's hoarding again, I need to catch her in the act."

"That's very thoughtful, Aly. I think. I'm getting this vibe that you're your mom's mom on some levels."

Alison reflected. "They grow up so fast, Paige."

"Okay, so you'll go over, share a grinder from Luke's, and organize her National Geographics from nineteen eighty-eight."

"Smithsonian, but yes. I'm going to organize them right into the trash."

Paige giggled. "Okay, but what if they spark joy?"

"Honestly, it's the candles that drive me crazy. She'll have, like, a cilantro lime candle and a lavender mint candle happening at the same time and I can't."

Paige reeled at the olfactory imagery and moved on. "So, you ditch mom's collectable Burger King Twilight cups, and swing by the party for the second act."

"She doesn't even like Twilight. I don't know why she has so many of those god forsaken cups. But, yes. Fine. And you said gathering."

"Gathering. It'll be small, I pinky promise."

"I'll swing by the gathering at nine and I'm leaving at ten forty-five."

"I accept your terms," Paige conceded. "You'll be glad you took the opportunity to unwind."

Alison laughed. "I never said I'd unwind. I'm gonna be so uptight!"

"Yeah?"

"Yeah, super uptight. And like, obnoxiously paranoid."

"I love that!" Paige was bordering on a snort classic but settled on a diet snort as she encouraged Alison's nightmare party persona.

"Yeah, you're going to be so glad you brought me. I'm gonna chew my potato chips at three hundred beats per minute and I'm gonna bring a loose bottle of hot sauce as a gift. I'll just present it to the hosts like a bottle of wine."

That pushed Paige into the true snort zone. "Jesus, Aly. You know, you're actually very socially savvy."

"Tell that to my anxiety."

"I know, I know. That's the trick, isn't it?"

***

Alison was feeling cautiously optimistic on the way to mom's, but a twinge of something-ain't-right ran up her spine as she crossed the walkway and approached the house. There wasn't even much of a difference. Just a thin layer of dust on the landing that shouldn't be there. She let the nervous shiver run its course and stopped with her hand on the doorknob for a too-long moment, knowing full well that she couldn't take it back once she opened it.

Then came the yipping. Two small, vaguely Yorkie-looking fur-demons completely lost their minds when they heard Alison's weight shift at the door. They scratched and yawped endlessly– not even stopping to check for ID when Aly opened the door. The transition to humping was seamless: one on each foot. She was extraordinarily distracted from the mission at hand. You know. Because of the humping. And the smell kind of crept up on her. The smell and the humping dogs and the disarray. Where in tarnation did she get the idea to add dogs into the mix?

The living room had exploded with clutter. Some of it disguised as order due to the neat stacks of DVDs, papers, and knick-knacks. But the uselessness of the items in question gave it away. Hard to make order out of junk that no one needs. There was an area for Amazon boxes that she wasn't ready to throw out. Three dog beds lined the throughway to the kitchenette. Perhaps one was the wrong size? Or there was a dog she hadn't found yet. Nothing would surprise her at this point. Except, actually, one thing did surprise her. Irene Ashe herself, stirring on the couch after an apparent nap.

The movement was really jarring to Alison because mum had been quite camouflaged by the chaos of the room. She had been napping on the couch, covered by two too-small blankets, her hand gently mothering a Big Gulp.

"Oh, honey! Hi," croaked mum through the end-haze of her midday repose. "I wish I had known you were coming. I'd have tidied up a bit."

Alison cried.

"Honey," Irene repeated, dropping her blankets as she deftly avoided the carefully stacked take-out boxes. She embraced her daughter, who couldn't move just yet, but allowed the comfort given.

Alison cried into her mother's loving shoulder as two long-forgotten ancestors of the mighty *Canis lupus* went to town on her ankles.

Eventually, she just started cleaning. Mom knew the drill. If they just kept cleaning, they wouldn't have to talk about it. Alison took advantage of the silence by taking an armful of boxes straight down to the trash. She did have to ask about the dogs, though.

"Went with boys, then?"

"They're brothers," mom replied, perking up at the

opportunity to talk about her new fur babies. "Met them both at the Humane Society. Well, the Humane Society Instagram. I couldn't separate brothers, could I?"

Alison failed to understand why not adopting them would somehow constitute separating them, but she let it go.

Irene continued "Aren't they sweet? Danny and Ascot."

"Ascot?" Aly questioned.

"Yeah, he keeps getting his you-know-what caught in the dog door."

This was a very Irene Ashe joke, and like all Irene Ashe jokes, it got her, lightening the mood considerably. They laughed together and resumed packing in silence, sans the extremely necessary Tokyo Police Club pumping its way through Alison's earbuds. The electrified brit pop channeled the nu punk simplicity perfectly, surely via an analog pedal and some extra tweedy amplifiers.

She needed the good vibes of the upbeat, catchy record if she was going to properly grin and bear the awkwardness of a mother-daughter cleanup sesh with strong "who's mothering who?" energy.

It was good to be back. However, something was itching her brain and she couldn't shake it. Something was sort of floating around in there that didn't add up. She had definitely seen mom slip into hoarding before. Nothing new there. Not entirely surprised that she got herself some company, though the quantity of the beasts was somewhat alarming. *Wait. That. Something about the dogs. Danny. And. Ascot.*

"Mom, how do you have a dog door?! You're on the second floor of an apartment complex."

Irene looked around like someone else was going to

answer. "Well," she started, buying herself some time to consider her wording for the tricky part. "I made a little yard out of the balcony." She gulped, big. "I got astro-turf."

Alison was on the move. This was beyond irresponsible.

"Mum, this is beyond irresponsible!"

A dog door was, in fact, fitted into the sliding glass door that led to the balcony. There was, in fact, a strip of astro-turf laid out, parallel to the black iron railing that confined the small space. It was littered with waste, solid and otherwise. The distinct smells of old and new urine danced together above the explosive olfactory sensation of ripe solid excrement. Alison downed the stairs and made a u-turn around a familiar, black banister towards the covered parking lot where she could catch a glimpse of the underside of mom's balcony, which also served as the upper face of the patio of the couple living below. Sure enough, a wet stain was beginning to darken through the concrete.

Irene followed after her to find her daughter gesturing to the discolored ceiling of the neighbor's patio. "You see that, mom? It's not just you that this stuff affects!"

"I know, I know. I'm sorry. I've just been so tired since–" An alarm went off on Irene's phone upstairs. She trailed off after it.

After the trek, she silenced the alarm and started preparing her insulin shot. Instinctively, Alison moved toward the supplies to help, but they were different now. Several of the disposable syringes had already had their tops twisted off, and were stopped by small sections of wine corks. Several other, larger, reusable syringes contained various amounts of the clear liquid. Irene injected herself with two of them, one a quarter-full, another half-full.

"You're rationing insulin?!"

"Insurance doesn't cover the whole dose anymore. It's fine. I'm at three quarters. And I do the full dose every other time."

"Mom! You cannot– absolutely cannot– ration insulin! Please, don't argue with me on this one!"

Irene sighed as Alison continued. "You can have the dogs. You're going to take them on five minute walks twice a day and I'm going to scrub the bejesus out of that 'yard' after we dismantle it. But you can keep the dogs, and I'll even babysit them sometimes when things get hard. You can have your magazines from three decades ago, and your insane candles, and you can have as many Big Gulps of half Diet Dr Pepper and half iced tea as you want. But you are not going to die to save thirty eight dollars a month on insulin. Okay?!"

Irene looked more tired than ever. "Okay. I'll call Dr. French on Monday morning. Maybe there's a local pharmacy or another plan or something."

"I'll call her, too, and follow up. Take that other quarter-dose."

"Okay."

***

Alison had developed a habit of silencing her phone when she visited mom. Between that and the shock of the new developments, she managed to miss 16 texts and four phone calls from Paige. The party was over. Paige wasn't happy about being stood up.

The last text read "The game is cool and all, but sometimes I just want a friend, you know?"

Alison breathed in sharply. She did know.

It had been about three minutes of idling in the carport before she realized she was home. She cut the engine, but she wasn't ready to move yet. A yellow light from the neighbor's porch gave her an eerie feeling, compounding the uneasiness of the day's new weight. The crumbling, baby blue paint on the siding became a soft sunburst of tawny and ember. She clicked off the headlights and let her eyes adjust again. Now she could detect the faint blink of the car's red quartz digital clock reminding her that it was always midnight.

"Guess I'll keep fighting," she blurted out without connecting the dots as to where that thought came from. *Where did that come from?* She gave it some air. It seemed like everything was some kind of fighting for Aly. She was fighting to keep her scholarship. Fighting to make rent. Fighting twice as hard as the country club kids for the same A minus that they got on pedigree. Theatre was fighting because the only thing she could excel at was stage combat. The game was fighting because she had to fight to be noticed, fight to be trusted, and then sometimes actually physically fight– usually against someone who could just glide through on natural strength alone.

Not Aly, though. Nope. Every win was tempered with fire. It was starting to get very tiring watching everyone around her start on third base and stroll to the plate, half the time on her own RBI. After all, she was working for below minimum wage so that someone else could profit off a product that was addictive on its own. "Don't worry," her supervisor told her. "You're so pretty, the tips will more than make up for it." Even at the bar, she was fighting her own self-interest by glaring at customers like a piranha at a fat thigh.

When you're poor, everything is fighting. Every intersection is against something meant to drain just a little more life out of you. Did you linger a little too long as you changed lanes? In a 2002 Camry, yes, you did. Don't be late with that fine, now, or you'll get your license revoked. That's okay, just take a day off work and school and go to the courthouse to get things cleared up. Just, don't drive there, obviously. Here's a fun game. Would you rather. Would you rather have the energy to make a healthy dinner, or have the money to pay for the ingredients? Would you rather have the water shut off, or the gas? Would you rather go to work sick, or use the fourth of your five yearly sick days before your pay starts getting docked? Meanwhile, Casey doesn't even get sick because he can afford to shop at Whole Foods and the cops never pull over new Land Rovers.

Alison sighed. "Okay, so my metaphor kind of ran out of gas there at the end." She removed a long hair clip, holding it to her face as a microphone as her sloppy bun fell to her shoulders. She smiled over the glasses she wasn't wearing to an audience that wasn't really there. "Just like my poor Camry." The audience roared. She shot a glance over to Jimmy Fallon, who was pounding his desk and fanning himself with his cue cards. He gestured to her to keep going.

"She's still got it, folks," he said, applause and laughter dimming as several whistles permeated.

"I'll be here all week, folks." She gave the audience a cute little smirk as they waited. "My eviction notice doesn't kick in 'till Thursday."

Jimmy wiped joyous tears from his eyes. "Alison Ashe, everyone. You can check out her fight scenes in Hamlet, March 1. We've got to go to break. Please listen to a few words from our sponsor, Nachos."

Alison was back in the car with the ominous yellow light and the blinking 12:00 and the existential dread. Maybe it was okay that she was tempered by fire. Maybe it was some kind of weird, twisted privilege if she looked at it the right way. For now, she needed to rest. And maybe some nachos.

FOURTEEN

Alison clutched her pearls.

"Oh, my!" she gasped, haughtily.

"Oh, my!" repeated Paige, mirroring Alison in word and gesture, but upping the ante slightly on intensity.

"Oh, rather!"

"Oh, my rather!"

Paige pushed Alison a little to the left as she ushered herself into the frame of the mirror they were sharing. Neither of them had worn pearls before, let alone clutched them, but they had to admit it was good fun. This was, of course, the point where the gag evolved into irreverence.

"My word, Lady Hall. Are you really going to the gala in that pauper's gown?" Alison asked, her Queen's English intensifying. "You don't expect to acquire a man in those rags."

Paige yes-anded. "Lady Ashe! Did you think this was a costumed masquerade? Are you going as the little match girl?"

"How's your husband, anyway? Still in prison for stealing that loaf of bread?"

An interstellar force shifted at that moment, bringing with it a certain cosmic balance. For just as light cannot exist without darkness, Paige Hall's now-classic snort was answered by a strange and otherworldly sonic disturbance emitted from dear Alison. It was an impish laugh, in the neighborhood of a cackle, but with soft, elven notes, a sly smile, and a glance that peered beyond this plane and into another world: a world where teacup handles had little bat wings on them. This laugh would come again– and when it did– it would be known as Alison's Goblin Laugh. Perhaps another day, the reader will become acquainted with Suzie Garcia's Horsey Sneeze, but that day is not today.

Even so, it was a big day for Suzie. Tonight was the grand opening gala for Renaissance Readymades, her series of oil portraits of the works of Marcel Duchamp. Included were various urinals signed by the infamous R. Mutt, a bicycle wheel seated on a stool, and her personal favorite, an exact black-and-white recreation of the Mona Lisa, but with a mustache. The gala would be a black tie affair, and would feature various performance art installations arranged by her good friend Alison Ashe. Most importantly, for both Suzie and Alison, the event was scheduled at the Altman Gallery in the Rockefeller Library. This meant a lot to Suzie, as her works would be displayed alongside Bauer's collection of Duchamp's pieces themselves, providing a fascinating contrast and reigniting the question "What is art?" The location meant a lot to Alison, too, because this was where the Chariot Raja was displayed– and tonight, she was going to steal it.

A college is a big place with many, many doors. Bauer, like many large operations, did not have a lot of uniformity when it came to limiting access to its doors. Some spaces had keycard access, others had numeric keypads from the decade before. Others still had regular old keys. Certainly, breaking into a restricted space was a move of questionable legality, not to mention judgement. Even so, it felt less bad for some reason to go for doors with numeric key-codes, as though accidentally guessing the right numbers somehow made it okay to be in a restricted area. By this logic, The Lord Chamberlain's Men identified a handful of key targets in the administrative and maintenance wings of Rockefeller Library, and sent the model asset to swipe the codes.

That asset was none other than Brian Ward: runner for our Footmen, all around cool guy, and, importantly, a very quiet person. Mind, a person can be quiet all day and still not be a quiet person. You can tell if a Kathy is going to be chatty. Not Brian Ward. He wasn't going to say a word unless it was absolutely necessary, and everybody knew it. Just ask him- he'll tell you all about it. Or he won't. In any case, he was pitch perfect for this mission. A clipboard mission. It is probably not news to this audience that a clipboard offers a special modicum of "I'm supposed to be here" energy. Combine that with a nice, quiet boy, and you've got yourself an invisible Brian. Aly sent him out on reconnaissance with instructions to wander around and write down codes. They say even the security cameras couldn't detect his presence.

It would not be entirely shocking to the casual observer that Alison was not a fan of dresses. After all, they had a hole in the bottom. Why? On this occasion, however, it wasn't exactly a dress, it was a costume. This was more than acceptable, it was exciting. She got to pretend to be the type of person who would dress fancy for a fancy dress party. Now, the color of the dress was another matter entirely. Grey dresses were hard to come by, so that was out. White? What is it, her wedding? Green? Prom. Blue? Prom. Red? Woah, buddy, cool your jets. So she wore a black dress, and lo, it was actually a cute look. Paige wore yellow. Paige looked good in everything.

"Shall we, darling?" asked Alison, applying the finishing touches on a big, black rose in her expertly pinned hair.

"We've quaffed, we've zhuzhed, we've fiddled. I think we shall!" Paige replied with the biggest smirk she owned.

"Fancy."

"Fancy."

"Fancy."

"Quite fancy."

The gala was about as fancy as an event on campus could be, all things considered. Two bars were stocked and gratis. The lights were moody, but not so low that you couldn't appreciate Suzie's art. A three-part jazz combination kept the mood in ¾ time, and the drummer even had those little metal brushes you see in the movies. They blended into the background like they were a permanent fixture. If they had been, it would make sense, anytime, day or night, for the Rockefeller was one of Bauer's proudest features. Red brick walkways and classic street lamps gave way to the black wrought iron fencing that encircled the long facade. Every angle was cut to the golden ratio, with perfect rectangles crosshatched within smaller, somehow more perfect rectangles to form the building cuts, courses, and windows. The walls crawled with real ivy. Within, exposed maple beams resembled a Viking longhouse. Glass walls enclosed study spaces that curved around corners as paths wound towards reading rooms, community spaces, and galleries. And all roads led to the stacks, which spilled into all other spaces, their mahogany majesty touching as far as the eye could see.

Upon Alison's request, there were also little men running around serving cocktail wieners. She said it was to make sure there was always movement during the operation, but everyone knew the truth: she was going to get hungry. They may have gone over budget on the wieners.

Aly and Paige strolled in, arm in arm, thirty one minutes late. This was late enough to qualify as fashionable, but early enough to make sure everything looked peachy. Even though she planned the whole thing, Alison was taken aback by the pomp and circumstance. It wasn't her style, but it was very fun to pretend that it was, if only for the night.

That reminds me, she thought, slipping an earbud into position and fiddling coolly with her phone. She flicked her music app deftly to favorites and grabbed Only for the Night, by Rx Bandits. A cacophony of flawlessly mixed et cetera exploded into her mind: horns, bass, loud guitars, and patently articulate drums. Everything slid into the musical space with an intensity and So-Cal chill that only Matt Embree and his bandits could dish out. His voice bled desperation and control at the same time as he wailed the fleeting loss of a moment in time. The song was beautiful and intense and short, like a play, or a year of college, or life.

Scanning the room, she found several faces to mingle with, and one she'd like to mangle. Reed Baker, her self-proclaimed nemesis, leaned against a low wall with a champagne flute. The wall was exactly elbow height, not terribly surprising in a world made for men that are five foot, nine and three quarters. He had his weight on one leg, the other in a practiced cross in front. He'd look just like a movie star if not for the red hair. Instead, he was a sort of voodoo doll of Conan O'Brien. Still, he seemed rather in place for someone that was not invited. She'd deal with him later, however. No need to ruin a perfectly good song.

The intrepid duo split at the foyer. Paige needed a drink to swish around and Alison needed about nine of those cocktail weenies before she was ready to schmooze. When they circled back, it was at the arm of the guest of honor.

Suzie Garcia wore an opalescent silver gown that sparkled prisms of red, gold, and green in the ambient light. Alison took a moment to finish the chorus of Karma Chameleon that was running in her head, and then greeted Suzie warmly.

"Fabulous series, darling!"

"Alison, thank you! I can't believe you threw such an extravagant opening for little old me!"

"Oh, it was the least I could do."

Paige chimed in here. "I can't think of a better way to celebrate women than to paint a bunch of urinals." Her audience giggled as she continued. "The Da Vinci piece, though. How did you even do that?"

"Oh, simple. I just did everything Da Vinci did and then everything Duchamp did, and then a little more."

"I'm sure you were paid just as well, too."

Alison laughed heartily, but her face fell into a deep grimace as Reed Baker elbowed his way into the conversation. She frowned, then checked her teeth for remnants of cocktail wieners, then unleashed a big fake smile. Her etiquette school skills were, in this moment, remedial.

"I just wanted to say," said Reed with his mid-Atlantic charm, "that your series is absolutely stunning."

Alison, who was absolutely stunned at the moment, was thankful that it wasn't her turn to talk, because she didn't have anything to say that wasn't deeply profane. She took the opportunity to scan the room for other known assets. Paige saw her cue and proceeded to keep Reed busy. Corners. Clear. East exit. Dalton was slipping into the men's room. Floor. Clear. Altman. Clear, as far as she knew. West stacks. Somebody studying in one of the cubes. Looked in-place, but nobody's going to study during a gala. Not when there's jazz playing.

"Excuse me a moment, Reed, is it?" she said as she slinked out of the circle.

"You know that it is."

"Do I?"

She did. A moment later and she was on the move, switching to coms as she fast walked. "Jeeves."

"Sir," chirped Teddy Dalton.

Alison enjoyed his prompt and eager response. "Can you get eyes on a study bug in the cubes at the west stacks?"

"Copy, sir. You had me at study. One cannot simply study when there's jazz playing."

Alison smiled a knowing smile. "Thank you, Jeeves. You'll have to–" but that was all she could say, for every conversation in Rockefeller Library ended abruptly at that moment.

It goes without saying that Bauer College's library was designed to facilitate a great number of activities simultaneously. This to meet the diverse needs of a wide body of students. Not many forces could disrupt a gala of this caliber in full swing. However, it may now be noted by the reader that a fifty-eight-piece marching band fully clad in urinal costumes and playing John Phillip Sousa's Stars and Stripes Forever could do the trick. The world stood still. Drums clattered with bawdy cadences. Trumpets blared. Trombones did that whoopty whoop thing that trombones do. And the urinals shone with the purity and innocence of sparkling ivory. The moon frowned in jealousy at their glimmering porcelain.

The players wove in and out in brilliant, choreographed procession as the partygoers parted to make room. The jazz combo, thrilled by the audacity and change of pace, joined in. We all knew they could play a song with a main idea if only they tried. The urinals twisted in delicate formation and intricate patterns, their song stealing the night with its catchy melody and upbeat resonance. As it crescendoed to its apex, the players closed in on the center of the gallery. They crowded so tightly that they began to step on each other. The central players each took a knee as the outer circle ascended, followed by a second layer to form a human pyramid. A single cymbal player rose to the center, lifted by an unseen force, and brought his two Zildjian Concertina Cymbals crashing together in explosive fury as the song came to a close, a huge smile emerging as he basked in the epicenter every partygoer's attention. The crowd went bananas.

As the band returned from whence it came, it occurred to Alison that Paige was still babysitting Reed Baker, and she moved to remedy that situation with haste. Paige, who seemed fine just walking away from her circle without saying a word, joined Alison alone near a particularly dramatic portrait of a bicycle wheel. Alison looked a little worried as she whispered something discreet to her compatriot. Paige smiled and nodded sweetly, jabbing Alison in the ribs with one hand and reaching into her handbag with the other. From the bag, she produced a tampon, which she quietly passed to Alison. Having no bag of her own, Alison tucked it into her armpit and moved at a modest pace to the bathroom, trying her best to hide a wave of mild embarrassment from her mannerisms.

One Aperol Spritz later, Alison's social endurance was starting to wane. She gave Paige a little nod and gestured towards the exit, and Paige sent back an eyebrow of understanding. Before she left, however, she was hoping to check in with Dalton about the wanton studier in the cubes. She took a beat and pulled him up on the coms as Paige made her final rounds. "Any word on the asset in the stacks?"

"Sir. I was able to snap a photo, but I have not yet matched his identity to any known assets. I'll keep trying. How goes the mingling?"

Alison sighed. "No sweat, Jeeves. Just packing up in the Altman. Paige is powdering her nose, and then we'll probably need some ice cream."

"Very good, sir. If you're going to Frosty Jane's, might I recommend the Double Dutch Bus?"

"You might, indeed, Jeeves."

Alison strolled towards the exit, making a point to keep a steady pace as Paige joined her. With the slightest motion, she opened the crook of her elbow, allowing her companion to lock arms with her as they crossed the threshold and wandered into the moonlight, whose silver beams were touched this evening with faint hints of green.

They rounded a familiar corner at Prospect and George, where they were bathed in warm lamplight from above. Paige lifted a small, white statuette into view so they could examine her handiwork a little closer. Alison smiled as she got her first good look at the Chariot Raja, its smooth, age-worn limestone features absorbing the wild energy of the night. She let out a deep breath and gave her friend a little squeeze, never breaking stride or calling undue attention. Paige slipped the statuette back into her clutch and they continued on into the cool night.

"What'd you end up putting on the pedestal in its place?"

"Bar of soap."

FIFTEEN

Dalton was right about the Double Dutch Bus. Soft, fluffy chocolate ice cream with a generous chocolate ribbon. It tasted like a Kinder Egg with another, melted Kinder Egg mixed in. And no nuts. Nuts in ice cream were an abomination. As far as Alison was concerned, there would be no crunchy in her smooth, end of story. Paige had Rocky Road. Paige was a maniac.

They walked in silence, Alison enjoying her ice cream, Paige enjoying her ice cream with nuts. The op wasn't over yet, but the evening had thus far provided a cavalcade of delightful shenanigans to reflect on. Truly a spectacular evening for all, but not everyone could enjoy it quite like Alison. For not everyone knew what Alison knew.

For example, not everyone knew that the Chariot assets from the Psychology Department relied on a SONAR system to monitor their Raja. Rockefeller had plenty of cameras, but they belonged to the college proper. It was actually a very difficult task to install security equipment in such a high profile space. For this reason, they kept it behind a hand dryer in the men's restroom, which shared a wall with Altman. This particular restroom also had a well-stocked paper towel dispenser, so there was no reason to touch, question, or notice a hollowed-out hand dryer. And no one did, until the day that a quiet, unassuming student employee with a clipboard gave the controls a shot. He hadn't been in a hurry that day anyway. During the gala, Teddy was able to make quick work of the device– not disabling it, but rather re-configuring it to a sensor that was far less likely to be disrupted. The salmon-tainted microwave in the Green Room at Leeds. A large strip of masking tape adorned that cursed microwave with a warning to those who would dare open it. It read "Peters cooks his nasty fish sandwiches in this microwave. You've been warned."

Another fact of the night's proceedings that not everyone knew was that The Lord Chamberlain's very own Brian Ward had three and a half years' experience in Marching Band, and took up the mantle again this very evening. His instrument: the concert cymbals. It was he who transported the Raja to its first hand-off in the central floor. It was he who rose to the center of attention atop the human pyramid. And he never took his hands off his cymbals. Instead, he escorted the Raja around in plain sight, displayed prominently in the bowl of his urinal costume, but with a small alteration: a little disguise. This was both a matter of professionalism as a musician and a test of Alison's theory that there are certain objects that polite society likes to pretend simply do not exist.

One such object is the humble tampon. When a properly socialized eye makes contact with a tampon in public space, it averts itself with great urgency. So offensive is this item to our delicate sensibilities that we are compelled to look away. We are embarrassed at the very idea that another member of the privileged classes saw us even witnessing it. Look away, Lady Abernathy, for within that cotton is an implement of Mephistopheles! No, we mustn't see that instrument of evil. That wicked witch's wand. So we make it invisible. We look away, and refocus our eyes to the beyond, like it was an ex at the grocery store, or our friend's weird dad. And so, when Brian Ward promenaded the prime objective through the gala, it was out in the open, albeit dressed in the sinister plastic that only tampons wear.

The Raja was then scooped up by none other than Paige Hall, who kept it in her clutch for safe keeping until the second hand-off. This was of course, in plain sight as well, neatly tucked into Alison's awaiting armpit. When she moved the objective to the water closet, it was to disable its GPS device with the electromagnetic pulse emitter that she had pinned in her hair. The one that had been disguised as a black rose. When she heard the telltale click of the GPS sputtering out of commission, she stashed the Raja in the hand dryer for Paige to snag on the way out. This particular dryer was in perfect working order, and she didn't really mind if the king had one last trip to the salon for a blowout before reaching his final destination.

There was one item of intelligence from this evening's affairs that Alison did not know, and it panged at the corner of her mind. Who was the study bug in the cubes? She glanced at her phone for signs of communication from her gentleman's gentleman. Blank. Except– in the reflection of the black screen, deep in the background, beyond the low shrubbery of College Street which they left behind over a block ago, she thought she saw something jiggly. And red.

"Jellybean!" shouted Alison as she took a hard left and

moved into a run. It was their special codeword, just for the two of them, and it meant it was time to move on to Plan B. Paige, shocked by the suddenness and volume, launched her ice cream over her shoulder with a tremendous "EEK!" It's always sad to lose a good cup of ice cream in battle. At least it was only Rocky Road. In case the reader is wondering, Alison had completed her Double Dutch Bus five minutes prior, as her ice cream journey was unimpeded by nuts.

After the minor fumble, Paige sprang into action, taking off to Alison's immediate right, but not before making a tremendous lateral pass of her handbag to her dear friend. Alison caught it deftly and they split up, sprinting opposite directions into the night.

Alison opened her gait into a full sprint, vaulting over a bench as she rounded the corner of Prospect and headed towards Watson Hall, where she could safely deposit the objective. She was faster than Baker and she knew it. Still, she didn't notice any of the telltale signs of being followed. She must have completely shaken him. Or worse: he wasn't after her at all. As she started to slow her pace to reconsider her position, Dalton buzzed into her coms.

"Sir. I've managed to identify the asset studying in the stacks. It would appear to be one Nicholas Rodgers."

Rodgers. Where had she heard that name before? *Wait– is that? Duffel coat!* That fink double crossed her!

"Okay, Alison, think!" she said to herself as she sputtered to a stop. *If Baker and Duffel are both in pursuit and I've shaken them, then– I'm not the target.* "Paige is!"

She snapped into a sprint, doubling back to Leeds, where she knew Paige was headed. It wasn't even a question. Yes, she could complete the op, opening a pathway for a Footman victory. But only if she left Paige to the sharks. There was no point. No point in winning without her friend. What good is an expensive bottle of champagne or a carne asada burrito from Nico's if you don't have someone to enjoy it with? Better to celebrate a loss with your best friend than a win without her. As her feet pounded and her heart raced, she knew she had made the right choice. She was going back.

As she closed in on the gardens outside of the theatre, she could see Baker standing in the lamplight, arms folded, looking on at two kneeling figures in the shadows beneath an arch of primrose.

"Miss Ashe, kind of you to join us," he said without moving as she approached.

"Jesus, Reed. Why do you have to talk like a movie villain?" she huffed as her flat feet slapped to a halt. As her eyes adjusted, she could now see Paige kneeling heavily on one knee. Nick Rodgers stood above her, twisting her arm behind her back in a wrist lock.

"You're hurting me!" Paige cried, clearly in pain from the hold. Alison could now see a tear in the knee of her leggings and a streak of road rash where she had slid, or been slid, into this position. As Rodgers held her wrist firm, he put downward pressure on her, forcing her torn knee further into the concrete. Alison's eyes darted quickly towards Paige's pin. Still intact. That was something.

"She's lying!" shouted Rodgers. "If I let up, she'll do some kind of twisty gymnast thing and kill me."

Paige's face contorted in pain. Her eyes were welling

up as she pleaded. "I won't! Just let up a little! You're–hurting– me!"

Reed turned his gaze toward Alison. "Maybe you should help your friend." Alison took a step towards the melee, but Reed put up a finger to stop her. "No, not like that," he said, calmly. "The Raja. Toss it here and you both walk free."

Alison froze. There was a lot to consider here. Baker had proximity to Paige, who was down. If she took to combat, he could take her pin before Alison could even try to take on two enemy assets at once. Was there any way out of this? Could she get the Raja out of the bag and just toss the bag? Not cleanly. Could she go after Reed without risking Paige's life? Maybe, but it would be messy and she could get hurt badly. The tree of possibilities branched out a thousand ways, and they all looked dark and uncertain. Except one. She breathed deeply and removed the figurine from Paige's clutch. She made eye contact with Reed and tossed it– to Rodgers.

From the trajectory of the toss, Nick Rodgers needed to take a full step to his left to catch it, preventing it from shattering on the concrete. This released his grip on Paige and she rolled out of his proximity. All four assets shifted away from each other and held their palms out, an unspoken gesture to indicate that the transaction was complete and that the violence was over, for tonight.

"Good enough," said Reed as he and Duffel backed away into the night. "Pleasure doing business, as always."

When they cleared, Paige sighed and started a path straight home. She was limping badly. Alison moved to help support her weight, but she batted her away, crying, "Don't touch me!"

Alison looked her friend in the eye. Both faces were dampened with tears. She opened her mouth to speak, but could only manage a single syllable.

"I–"

"Do you have any idea how long you just stood there?!"

Alison stayed silent, mouth agape, trying to speak but nothing came out. Paige limped over to a bench facing Waterman Street and produced her phone as she sat.

"I'm gonna call a car. I need you to give me some space right now, okay?"

Alison could feel a huge cry coming, but quelled it for the moment so that her friend would know that she was going to honor the request.

"I understand," she said, and walked away.

When Alison rounded the corner of Waterman and Thayer, she let it out.

Alison walked home, passing hallowed campus landmarks and beautifully aged Brownstones and perfectly trimmed oaks and sweetly lit gardens. Instinctively, she slipped in her earbuds and popped open her music app. Instead of her typical, thoughtful search for the perfect song, she just typed a "P" for Paige. Her top result was a familiar sketch of a dejected cheetah: the cover of Viva Last Blues by Palace Music. Her thumb hovered over New Partner for a long time before she could bear to select it. The slide guitars and brushed drums immediately brought dark clouds rushing into her mind. The strained lyrics and melancholy harmonies brought a rain that washed everything else away.

SIXTEEN

When Alison had turned around and gone back for Paige, it had become so clear to her why she played Chaturanga. It was an excuse to spend quality time with her friend. To share something unique and special. Maybe that's not why she started, but it was definitely why she kept going. So it stung especially that things were going to be different now. She'd seen it many times: that look we give when things go sour. And she saw it in Paige the night before. It killed her to sit in the uncertainty of how Paige would respond, but she also wasn't about to smother her with texts. No, when someone asks for space, the ball's in their basket, or whatever the sports metaphor was.

After a bout of doom scrolling, Alison realized her phone wasn't going to do anything on its own, so she tried to keep herself busy. She went for a run, aggressively cleaned her room, the kitchen, and bathrooms, and even resorted to getting her homework done. On time. None of it made her phone buzz.

"Alright, then, phone. If that's how you wanna play, then that's how we're gonna play. I'm going for a hot dog."

Alison's phone said nothing.

"In New York!"

She flipped the device into a spinning baton motion, letting it rotate a few times in the air before swatting it into her clothes hamper. Then she turned on her heel and left the room, slamming the door. A few moments later, she came back for her keys, repeated her tantrum, and slammed the door again. She had almost made it to the front door when she turned around a second time.

"Don't get any ideas, I'm just coming back for some CDs."

Once properly on the road, she took a breath and smiled cathartically. She had a few wordless thoughts to muster up her feelings at the moment, but the only idea that could form a sentence was "That'll show him." Apparently, her phone was a boy.

The endless snow-capped conifers made beautiful patterns in the distance as the interstate twisted and turned. Flashes of green needles jumped out amongst the snow and earthen tones of giant rock formations. There was a certain lull to the lonely drive that made Alison feel at peace. One hill climbed to reveal verdant mountains and new vistas on the horizon, only to be hidden again after the steep drop-off and smooth corners. She flipped back and forth between the four CDs she had scooped out of her end table drawer. All of them, she decided, were going to make her cry, so she might as well just grab one. She looked away and grabbed one at random. It was Rooney's 2003 self-titled album.

"Dang," she said as she swung open the cracked jewel case. "This one's gonna make me cry."

Despite several ballads on the way up, she held it together until track six: I'm Shakin'. The poppy, upbeat four-four drums, the laid back surfer guitar licks, and just the general contagious energy caught Alison by surprise as she began to bounce around, shift gears in time to the beat– not recommended– and sing along in her mad voice. It couldn't be helped. The catchy, delicious Nor-Cal vibes took hold, and she was transformed.

Technically, she didn't cry until after the song. Maybe it was just so fun that it broke the emotions loose. Maybe it was the lyrics that reminded her that we all have trouble sleeping when we're having a hard time. Maybe she was just due for an unspecified cry. Anyway, it happened, and it passed. And she drove four and a half hours to New York City for a hot dog.

Honestly, it was a really good hot dog. And while we're being super honest, it was actually three hot dogs. Two for now and one for later. The ol' New York Pocket Dog. Alison wandered around Times Square for an hour or two with her pocket dog and some ice cream– it was no Frosty Jane's but it would do– when she stumbled upon an obnoxious neon installation. Upon further inspection, it turned out to be a silent disco. This was in fact the perfect introspective activity: day-glo cyberpunk decor, loud music pumped direct-to-brain via headphones, and lots of people but they can't talk to you. The music was actually better than expected. She bopped around to Franz Ferdinand and The Kooks while she finished her pocket dog and took in the faces that she'd never have to see again.

At two AM, she awoke in her car, a fine puddle of drool amassing in the space between her shoulder and the car seat headrest. "Hey, just like the Rooney song said I would. A prophecy foretold!" She looked around to find the streets no less alive than they were in the waking hours. Feeling kind of rested, she released the parking brake and headed back to New Haven, taking just a quick second to make sure all four CDs she brought were still in the passenger seat. They were undisturbed. In fact, she had buckled them in. "Safe as houses. Not gonna let anything happen to you, Tragic Kingdom."

Returning to her home at nearly seven AM, Alison zombie walked up the stairs to her room and face-planted into her bed, still strapped into her cutest pair of jeans. And then it was 9:30. She had done it! Twelve hours of no phone. When she dug it out of the hamper, she found a voicemail from a 401-number and a text from Paige. It read "Hey, girl. I think I need a little break from the game. I'm so behind on my classes and my lines and I just need to try and come up for air. Let's check in after Hamlet and I'll let you know where I'm at."

This was incredibly reasonable, all things considered. Alison had run through a number of possible conversations in her head on her drive. She thought about defending herself and begging Paige not to be mad at her. But she knew Paige wasn't really mad at her. She was overwhelmed– by boys and privilege and Hamlet and school and a badly scraped knee. She tore a calendar off the wall and flipped it to the next page. Opening night was in three weeks. She sighed one of those horsey sighs. Three weeks with no Paige! Dang, that was going to be rough. She drafted about forty responses before landing on "Totally understand xxox." She felt good about that text. It was a good text.

Keeping busy for three weeks was actually quite doable with midterms and mom tending, office hours with Cap'n Casey, production meetings and tech rehearsals. The list went on. A fresh day upon her, Alison decided to eat the biggest frog first. She made an appointment with Dr. French to figure out her mother's dosage and insurance. As luck would have it, they had a cancellation at four. Irene made Reubens for lunch and watched Harold and Maude with her daughter before they jumped into the Camry to sort out the endless battle between capital and inalienable human rights which seemed to become more alienable lately. Dr. French played around on her computer until she found a brand and dosage and monthly schedule that wouldn't murder her patient or force her into homelessness. Alison made a huffy speech about the extra administrative burden most likely leading to too many patients getting railroaded into one of those outcomes or the other. The good doctor laughed sardonically in agreement, wishing quietly that there was more she could do about it.

On Monday, Alison wrote a painfully mediocre essay about the limited access to union membership for Hollywood stunt performers and how they might fare better on the New York stage if only they could find a place in Staten Island and didn't mind the commute. And of course, move across the country and leave their families and friends behind and stuff.

On Tuesday, she had another practice in her office with Casey Harrington. He had improved quite a bit, much to her surprise. Something about his energy seemed less floppy and dangerous than it had before. He seemed significantly more in control than in previous workouts. His knaps were on time, his spacing was good. He looked kind of on-schedule to avoid knocking out Laertes on opening night.

"What's up, Casey? That was a really good exchange. You been practicing at home?"

Casey smiled. "Yeah, sort of." He looked a little embarrassed. After a beat, he continued. "So, I was thinking about our last conversation, about not knowing my own strength and stuff. And, I went to visit my parents, and I was watching Mr. Rodgers on PBS with my little sister, Sammy. She's seven."

Alison nodded, not about to interrupt him during his most introspective monologue yet.

Casey went on. "So, on the show, he gave one of the boys an egg to carry around because he had accidentally been too rough with his friends. And Sammy was like 'Casey, you should try that!' So we got an egg, and I've had it in my backpack ever since." He went over to his backpack and, from the front pocket, produced a bright yellow egg with a little face drawn on it and a tail shaped like a lightning bolt on its backside.

Alison giggled. "Why is it Pikachu?"

Casey blushed a little. "Sammy likes Pikachu. She made me promise not to hurt him. It actually helped. I gotta be careful with the little guy. She'd be devastated if I squished Pikachu."

Alison smiled again. It was a really nice outcome. She had influenced someone! "Wow, Case. That's– that's really– NICE." She had really landed hard on the last word. There was an unusual gruffness in her voice which made Casey laugh. It was good to have something to humanize him. Something to give him an anchor. Although lord knows he had enough anchors in his wardrobe. Still, it was, to quote a great fight director, really NICE.

On Wednesday, Alison met with The Lord Chamberlain's Men. They were down to three. Dalton and Ward filled two other chairs reserved for assets. Peters took up the large recliner. Paige's chair remained empty.

"She's not dead," Alison blurted out as the first topic of business. "She just needs a little space from Chaturanga while she gets ready for Hamlet." Her teammates nodded in understanding as she continued. "She also got banged up pretty badly on the op. It was a darker side of the game that we haven't really seen thus far."

Control chimed in here. "We try to keep the gentlemen's agreement that hand-to-hand combat should avoid unnecessary cruelty. However, our esteemed engineers have been stepping on the toes of that agreement in recent years."

Dalton's knuckles were digging into his armchair as he processed this. "Elephants," he said, exasperated.

Peters took over again. "Did Baker and company walk away with the Raja?"

"Yes," said Alison, plainly.

"Do we have it on good information at this juncture that Nick Rodgers is working for the Elephant faction?"

"Yes."

Peters smiled. "Then, good chaps, we may count ourselves with another victory, for information is everything in these affairs."

Before Alison could protest, the three merry gentlemen were banging their palms on their armchairs in thunderous applause. Puzzled, but not to be outdone, she gave her chair a few good slaps as well. "I don't know how you boys remain so positive when we're in last place and falling."

"Sir," said Teddy Dalton, his baritone voice carrying a calming air. "Last place is a very special place to be in. Only from last place do we have nothing to lose."

On Thursday, Alison remembered that she still had a voicemail on her phone from her solo trip to Pocket Dog City. She was in class when she made this realization, and wasn't about to step out just to hear some telemarketer. At top of the hour, she wedged her phone between her shoulder and her ear as she plopped two bananas and some dry cereal on her tray in the South Dining Hall.

"Hey, Alison!" it started. Then the words went blurry, as though some sort of spell was preventing her from understanding them. She registered the vaguely familiar woman's voice and friendly tone. But the words themselves just suddenly didn't have any meaning. Like the voice on the other end switched languages somehow, though Alison knew she hadn't. It ended with "Break a leg, honey. I know you can do it!" A heartening sentiment, but for what? She sat down and worked on one of her bananas and decided to give it another try. But she was hesitating. Something seemed– off. She shook off the haze and popped her phone open again. This time she would focus on what this person was trying to tell her.

"Hey, Alison! It's Annie Watts. Listen, I have some bad news. Well, bad for me, but could be good for you, I think! I have mono, and I'm just not going to be able to take any chances with doing Ophelia. They say that symptoms can last for like, months. I feel like old soup. Anyway, I talked to Peters about it and we agreed that you should take on Ophelia. So sorry for the timing of all this, but, I guess that's why we have understudies! You're such a good actor, so I know you're gonna be great. Break a leg, honey. I know you can do it!"

SEVENTEEN

"My aim is true," Alison Ashe whispered to herself as the lights came up in the historic Leeds Theatre on opening night. It was a little mantra she liked to say to herself when she wanted to summon the strength to push through. The phrase came from the title of an Elvis Costello album. A beautiful and sad and strange album, and notably, one that her mother was extremely fond of. It helped, as did the secret earbuds and mood playlists, the five tenets of the Lord Chamberlain's Men, the secret code names, talking like old British dudes, and of course, plenty of opportunities to engage in hand-to-hand combat with other nerds on campus. Chaturanga had served Alison well this year. It had provided her with a beautiful distraction from an intense and formative period of her life. It was a creative outlet: one that really gelled with her personality– not an easy thing to find. And, perhaps most importantly, it was a vehicle for the development of a lifelong friendship with Paige Hall. Except, she wasn't sure about that last part right now, and waiting to find out was torture.

Luckily for Alison, she had zero time in the last three weeks to do anything but cram for a leading role in the most acclaimed play of all time. She'd been Ophelia's understudy all along, she could have learned some of the lines. Instead, she had been running secret operations, planning galas, and throwing bloody shoes at vicious sporks. Actually, some of that was a relief. Alison liked it when her troubles were her own fault. She didn't have to wonder who to blame or practice sticky hypothetical conversations at two AM. So, with the privilege to self-deprecate in hand, Aly was in the driver's seat to figure out how to get a whole Ophelia into her brain in 1.5 fortnights. As she wasn't exactly sure how to pull this off, she was delighted that she didn't have time to think about it. Peters arranged extensions for her classwork, she was called to extra rehearsals, she still had all of her design responsibilities, and if there was a free moment, she used it to furiously memorize her lines. Right now, with the most important thing on the line– keeping her friendship with Paige– she embraced the chaos, took comfort in it. Even so, a little Elvis couldn't hurt.

Paige was either being distant and weird or she was giving Alison the space she needed to prepare for her role in record time. Either way, they didn't interact much at rehearsals or backstage. Passing ships in the night and whatnot. It was fine. Paige had a lot to work on as well with her role. Horatio was nothing to sneeze at. There also wasn't a lot of on-stage overlap between the two characters, so when one of them was backstage, the other was on. Alison shrugged it off. Something she learned from the game and her switch to BFA Tech and the absolutely insane year she'd just endured was that nothing usually means nothing. Which is to say, if someone doesn't text you, they're not intentionally trying to make you spiral. They literally didn't do anything. Gotta let it go.

In that spirit, Alison did herself a huge favor on the night before opening. Inspired by the silent disco she had surprisingly really enjoyed in the city, she decided to commandeer Leeds that evening for a solo dance party. As the final dress rehearsal ticked to an end, Alison stowed away in the lighting grid, crouched in a little basket with her script. Rehearsal was rather beautiful from all the way up there in her little crow's nest. She might have even been distracted by everything going on if not for the fact that she was deeply engaged in cramming as many lines into her head as would fit.

When the lights went out and the doors clanked shut, the theatre was all hers. She climbed down into the booth and powered up the lights and sound, connecting her phone to the main system via Bluetooth. She cued the lighting board over to Act IV, Scene V. Though this was technically her death sequence, Alison wasn't being dramatic. She just liked the cool blue wash of lights in that particular cue. She hiked down to the stage as she thumbed her music app over to favorites and selected a playlist entitled "I'M NOT BEING DRAMATIC, YOU ARE." She smiled deeply from her azure spotlight as the first notes of Sovereign Light Café by Keane rang triumphantly across the music hall. The juicy power-pop ballad was a wall of sound, exploding with chunky synthesizers, booming kick drums and bass that she could feel in her chest, and a silvery hue of emotional resonance laced with a glaze of sweet nostalgia. Keane was the only band Alison knew that could make her laugh and cry and dance at the same time, and she was due for all three.

Alison spent the next hour doing silly fake ballet twirls, vaulting across the stage, and shadow boxing. As she danced and played to the music, she recited some of her most challenging monologues. While this exercise was mostly just for fun, there was method in the madness, too. The songs, the lights, the silly dance moves, all made imprints in Alison's memory, helping her lock in those lines one last time. Her ears ringing and her heart pounding, she slept hard and dreamed weird. When she awoke at 11:28 the next morning, she knew her lines. Great, now all she had to do was– everything else, with no room for error. "When I grow up," Alison told herself on the way to the dining hall, "I'm gonna do something with room for error."

From the wings, she watched as Bernardo successfully tackled the first line of the show: "Who's there?" He nailed it. 10/10. Sold. That was a guard who definitely heard a noise. Alison paused her inner-snark-monologue and took a breath. The show had definitely started. No turning back now. As that reality sunk in, she double-checked that her headphones were tucked into her dress and that her college pin was visible. Even in period costumes and a full house at Leeds, Alison wanted to honor the rules of the game. In this moment, in the safety of the shadow of the heavy, black curtains, she started to take in the beauty of the production that she and her compatriots had poured their hearts into. The production design was gorgeous. The sets and costumes had been truncated to limited palettes. The only colors on stage were crimson, cerulean, onyx black, and gold. This gave the show a distinctive punch to it. The style was period-perfect Renaissance except for that detail. But it made all the difference. The skewing of the visible spectrum added an air of working with limited tools. It was Punk Renaissance, and she loved it.

As Casey started to get his sea legs, Alison noticed something else that she hadn't expected. He was getting laughs. At first, she figured it was just her reactions that the audience was responding to. After all, it was an acceptably impossible task to hear a boy from an Ivy League sailing team tell her to "Get thee to a nunnery" and not break the fourth wall with a stink face. That laugh might have been hers, but he was swinging above his weight on scenes that Aly wasn't even in. And they were eating it up. Funny Hamlet. That was her idea. How was it sneaking into this production? *Peters! That son of a cummerbund read my paper and decided to make Hamlet funny!* Now, that was an honor. Peters knew what he was doing. Alison also knew Peters wasn't the type to borrow an idea without giving credit, so he must have wanted to keep it a surprise. Dang, that felt good. Hiding little surprises in your art for your favorite people to find. Alison didn't know exactly what she wanted out of adult life, but she was sure that that was going to be a part of it.

She watched in awe and gratitude as Hamlet laid into King Claudius about the whereabouts of Polonius, whom he had recently murdered.

"Not where he eats, but where he is eaten. A certain convocation of politic worms are e'en at him. Your worm is your only emperor for diet. We fat all creatures else to fat us, and we fat ourselves for maggots. Your fat king and your lean beggar is but variable service—two dishes but to one table. That's the end." Casey was a decent actor, but Alison knew that he'd only put mustard on a line like that if someone told him to. And the crowd ate it right up. She was so excited about being in Hamlet: The Comedy that she almost missed her next cue. It was IV-V, where Ophelia goes crazy and drowns herself in the river. Well, if the audience wanted funny, she could make that funny. Gotta give the people what they want.

In all the whirlwind of the last few weeks, Alison had yet to have an opportunity to simply take the show in. She'd take it now, from the wings. A moment she very much deserved, as she was a designer for this production. The front cover of the Playbill would say "Fight Director: Alison Ashe." And that meant– that meant. *Oh, crud. That meant that mom was in the audience.* That's okay. If it goes terribly wrong, she and mom would have something to laugh about later. Lord knows they had spent many hours laughing together about things that went sideways in plays.

Truth be told, Alison wouldn't remember much about her performance that evening. Even in a big role, what she was really focused on was the fights. As Hamlet squared off against Laertes, Alison ran the steps quietly to herself from the wings. She had been a choreographer and a coach and, surprisingly, a mentor who had helped a trust fund brat to tread a little more lightly. She was proud of Casey Harrington as he kept his speed in check, even on opening night. His knaps looked good, his combinations looked strong. She even reeled at a haymaker she'd seen a thousand times before. Even knowing that it was fake, it looked like it packed a wallop. Wow. That meant she'd done a good job. What was this feeling? Pride? *Nice.*

There was another reason that Alison wouldn't really remember the quality of her Ophelia on opening night, and that's because in Act V, Scene I, something went wrong.

It all started out fine. Hamlet did his little piece with the gravedigger. Ophelia's coffin was placed center-right. Ophelia was already dead, so Alison didn't have any hard work left to do. Her only remaining responsibility was to let the pall bearers carry her to her coffin and lower her in. She laid limp as the four boys carried her on stage, her only struggle at this point was refraining from making a joke about all the attention. Her eyes were closed when Laertes opened the coffin, so her only indication that something was amiss was the collective gasp from the audience. The coffin, it turned out, wasn't empty.

"What is he whose grief bears such an emphasis, whose phrase of sorrow conjures the wand'ring stars and makes them stand, like wonder-wounded hearers? This is I, Hamlet the Dane."

But it wasn't Hamlet. It was Reed Baker, rising from Ophelia's coffin, dressed as Hamlet's father's ghost.

EIGHTEEN

Alison recognized Reed's voice immediately. She knew his game as well. He was banking on Alison's commitment to the craft: that she'd stay dead because "the show must go on." Unfortunately for Reed Baker, Alison had no such commitment to her art. She opened her eyes, looked straight out to the audience, and winked. The entire packed house of Leeds Theatre gasped collectively, with one exception. Suzie Garcia, who, when nervous, agitated, or exposed to a burst of sunlight, was capable of emitting a special, very loud sneeze that released so much air, energy, and detritus that her lips fluttered uncontrollably in its wake. This was Suzie Garcia's Horsey Sneeze. It's not important to the plot, but it happened, and the reader was promised that we'd get back to it, so there you go.

The pall bearers, apparently shocked by Ophelia's return to life, dropped her like a sack of bricks. She thudded appropriately, but didn't wallow for long. Instead, she rolled her weight to her upper back, folded her palms to the hardwood, and kipped to her feet. Unknowingly to Alison, this would set off a chain reaction that added a second layer of confusion to the already bizarre scene. For when Alison was dropped, her headphone cord was released from her phone, and, in the motion of her kip-up, she had apparently instructed it to continue playing her "I'M NOT BEING DRAMATIC, YOU ARE" playlist. Her phone was still happily connected to the Leeds Theatre Bluetooth system, and this fact entitled the audience to the perfect cuing of This fffire by Franz Ferdinand. They couldn't have timed it more perfectly if they had tried.

As the wild energy of electric guitars bounced against each other and the pulsing dance beat kicked in, Alison squared off. Reed, not wanting to be foiled by Ophelia's awakening, took to the weapon rack and produced– well, actually, a foil. Aly leapt directly to Hamlet's scabbard and removed his epee, pointing it at her opponent and then bringing the hilt to her lip in the French salute. She then gave the audience a mischievous look and spoke to them directly.

"And that's when Hamlet realized he was having a dream. A very groovy dream, from another time."

Reed didn't like this, and protested accordingly. "No, it wasn't a dream. It was Hamlet's dead father's ghost taking arms against his dead girlfriend."

But Alison was too quick for him. "That's exactly what a dream ghost would say," she retorted, and the audience roared. She moved in to attack, a lazy cut to the thigh, intended to be parried. Reed didn't disappoint. The blades rang against each other with a satisfying crash. Alison followed up with some footwork and a few other easy passes as the song's vocals splashed into the fray. The rest of the players were super confused at this point and did what confused actors do: backed away slowly for *whatever this was* and didn't break character. As the chorus thundered in, Alison exploded into a flurry of blows that Reed was helpless to defend.

Some of the strikes clattered against his foil while others simply thudded against his pumpkin pants. Alison smirked a little at the thought that she was literally whipping his bum. In the booth, Freddy Dennis had the sense to fade the music after the first chorus– not out of frame– just lower so that the audience could focus on the action of this apparently brand new scene. Ellie Foster followed suit with the lights, letting them bloom a little to intensify the fight. She also threw in some violet, since Alison had stated that it was a dream sequence. It is worth noting that the audience got a good laugh out of the bum whips. Perhaps a snort also sounded from somewhere in the deep recesses of the theatre. One can never tell when there's so much going on.

Reed Baker, who was starting to feel outmatched– because he was– decided to play to his strengths. In this case, there wasn't much to lean on, except his physical strength. He allowed one last whip in the pumpkin pants before grabbing the epee by its blade. Though this would historically be considered by many to be a bad move, it was fine in this setting because they were stage weapons. Reed tugged hard and pulled Alison into a grapple. He managed to get a hand on her wrist and a second wrapped around her back. She lunged, but not to get out of the grapple, it seemed. Somehow, it appeared she wanted to pull the melee down-center, a little more directly into the spotlight. Actors, am I right?

Reed could feel himself gaining control as Alison dropped her weapon and winced. He kicked out her right shin and she went down hard on the other knee.

"You know what's sad?" said Reed as he adjusted his grip on her wrist and snatched the other. "If you had gone after us at the garden arch, you would have had a fighting chance. Wanna know why?"

"Enlighten me," Alison coughed as Reed shifted his weight and her back crashed to the stage floor.

Reed went on as he finished the pin, leaving Alison helpless under his weight. "Elephant was running a short roster this year as well. So short, the whole agency was yours for the taking that night. You're good, kiddo. You're strong and you're smart. But we're a little stronger and a little smarter and we gotcha this year."

Reed Baker had his hands on her wrists in a perfect pin. She wriggled every errant muscle she could think of, hoping to find any sort of leverage, but there was none to be found. That was that. She sighed and eased downward, giving Reed a little nod to let him know that he'd won, though she was still too ashamed to make eye contact. She looked away, up into the cool blue lights and she awaited her fate.

"Any last words?" asked Reed, a devilish smile growing on his wicked but somehow still very cute face.

"Just one."

"Say it, then."

"JELLYBEAN!"

And reality collapsed. An otherworldly explosion of wood and metal bellowed through Leeds Theatre, its shockwave echoing against every wall, every surface– its resonance reverberating in every bone of every body. The floor tore open below them in an earth-shattering clamor. Reed Baker and Alison Ashe were free falling into the gaping maw of the earth itself, twisting and writhing towards its welcoming, molten core. And then, a *flumph*, and a thud, and a groaning cough, as Reed got the wind knocked out of him.

He was on his back now, in some sort of dungeon, perhaps. He wasn't sure. His eyes and his brain were still adjusting. Below him, something soft and leathery. Above him, Alison Ashe, who had somehow switched places with him as they fell and was now happily sitting on his chest. As he opened his mouth to speak, he heard the twist and click of his college pin detaching from its base. As the tunnel vision subsided, another figure materialized. It was Paige Hall, gripping a large lever on the opposing wall and grinning wildly. Mouth agape, he glanced down at the empty base of the pin, and back up at Alison, who was admiring the beautiful elephant etched on its underside. He had had something to say but instead held it in. Dead people don't talk.

Alison popped up off the crash pad and ran to Paige for a big, big hug. Alison's eyeballs might have popped out, the little devil squeezed so hard. She lifted her small-framed friend high in the air and spun, both giggling with joy and fury as the lights and music faded from above and Peters's voice came onto the intercom.

"We will now have a brief, fifteen minute intermission."

Reed was still lying there on his back, his hands tucked behind his head and a big smile on his face. Their joy was infectious and, if there was one thing he liked more than winning, it was losing fair-and-square to a worthy adversary. If you aren't going to win, it's time to root for your nemesis, if you're lucky enough to have one.

Paige and Aly hopped up onto the crash pad and sat cross-legged. Paige spoke first.

"Now that we've got a captive audience, I think it's time you knew that we got you. But not today, not three weeks ago. All the way back."

Reed looked confused. Or perhaps that's just what his face looked like. Alison chimed in. "Perhaps Mr. Baker requires a visual aid. Nicholas, why don't you come say hello to our little friend?"

The squeal of an old green room door, and Nick Rodgers emerged from the shadows beyond. "Hi, Reed." Reed sat up now and crossed his legs as well. He didn't speak, but he did laugh heartily and clap his hands together with glee. Nick gave a little bow as Paige jumped into the conversation.

"That's right, boyo. You were TRIPLE-CROSSED!"

"You see," Alison continued, "Rodgers was genuine in his commitment to Elephant losing this year. So genuine, in fact, that he changed majors so he could join you."

"And plant the idea in your head to run a short roster," said Nick.

Alison went on. "So, from the planning phases of the gala, we had always intended for you to walk away with the Rajas. All of them. So they'd be safe and sound when Elephant went dark."

Reed clapped again. His face went a little sour as a thought came across it. Unable to articulate this, because he was dead, he simply pointed at Paige's knee.

"Oh, that," said Paige. "We planned that, too. Aly taught us the whole exchange."

Reed made an odd spurting gesture with his fingers, perhaps to mimic blood coming out of her knee.

"Ah, yes. You saw me bleed. But did you hear the ketchup packet exploding from beneath my leggings? Did you smell the sweet Heinz Fifty Seven in the night air? I did. It was gross. I threw those leggings away."

Alison took over again. "Everything was designed for you to think you were one step ahead. The gala, the Rajas, the compromised coms, we even gave you an empty coffin and you just crawled right into it. And our buddy Nick Rodgers, well, he only had one condition for all his assistance. He wanted to be the one to snuff out the Elephant Faction once and for all. You ready, Nick?"

Nick nodded and took a deep breath. Then, he reached for his own token, and twisted it off with a satisfying click. Reed Baker clapped his little hands raw as Aly and Paige popped off the crash pad for their biggest hug in at least three weeks.

Baker was dead. Rodgers was dead. Ophelia was dead–not Aly though! But Horatio still had a scene to finish. Alison escorted Reed and Nick to the booth, where they could watch Act V from a couple of stools. From there she climbed up to her little crow's nest in the grid, and watched the rest of the show, grinning 'till the very end, despite all the murder and tragedy and stuff.

The audience gave a decisive standing ovation. Funny Hamlet was apparently a hit, and the patrons responded so well to the new dream sequence that they decided to keep it in. The front-page headline in the next day's Bauer Daily Herald would read "Hamlet Slays!"

Having made the switch to technical theatre, Alison had worried that she'd have to miss out on the thrill of acting. There was a certain rush to solving problems in-character, embodying the language and emotion so fully that she could think as someone else, take over, and make the call as to how they'd adapt to new and unknown circumstances. Tonight, that worry faded. Acting was everywhere. These skills she had honed and sharpened all her life would be of use in many challenges to come, whether on or off the stage. After all, she had just pulled off a performance of a lifetime, and it wasn't Ophelia.

Alison had lived and breathed a three-week friend breakup with her favorite pumpkin in the whole world. The entire charade had been Paige's idea, who remembered that Alison's phone had been compromised by the Elephants back in August, when she got Tony killed by sending him an intelligence photo on an unsecured line. Unsure of how sophisticated the enemy surveillance was, they had agreed to live the breakup, play through it as though it were really happening. If the Elephants bought it, perhaps they could be lured in to try and pick one of them off in their moment of weakness. You can count on an Elephant to try and kick you when you're down. Apparently, the bait is tempting enough that you can get him to sneak into a coffin. Even though it was premeditated, Alison was shocked by how real it had felt. Being away from your best boo was nothing to sneeze at. Even pretending to put a wedge between them drove Alison to real tears, and a real need to drive to New York City for a hot dog. Okay, okay, okay. Three hot dogs.

There was a lot still to figure out for Alison Ashe as she started to put together the pieces of her future. The heavy fog of uncertainty for what lay ahead used to really bother her. If she couldn't plan every moment, be in control of every detail, she'd fret and sweat and turn in her sleep and make flowcharts to plan her next move. But tonight, she started to feel that weight fall away, just a little. Because, whatever happened next, she knew she had one thing absolutely, undoubtedly, locked in. No matter what.

From the safety of their favorite booth at Frosty Jane's, Alison Ashe and Paige Hall giggled uncontrollably.

ALISON'S PLAYLIST

There are a few fun things going on in this book. My favorite little motif is Alison's deep connection to music and the little passages about the songs that she's listening to as she gets wrapped up in world of Bauer College's underground spy games. Since these are real songs, I thought it might be nice to share the playlist, so y'all could listen through her adventures on your next trip to the ice cream shoppe or roller rink. I'll make an official Spotify playlist and share the link. And, for you old-fashioned, no-internet folks (how are you reading this?), I'll write out the songs and artists and you can make a mix tape.

Alison's Official Spotify Playlist

Accidents Will Happen- Elvis Costello and the Attractions

Be Calm- fun.

My Time- Minus the Bear

Australia- The Shins

Bloody Mary- Silversun Pickups

At Night in Dreams- White Denim

Common People- William Shatner & Ben Folds

Genghis Khan- Miike Snow

Nancy From Now On- Father John Misty

House Fire- Someone Still Loves You, Boris Yeltsin

Club Foot- Kasabian
Breakneck Speed- Tokyo Police Club
Only for the Night- Rx Bandits
New Partner- Palace Music
I'm Shakin'- Rooney
Sovereign Light Café- Keane
This fffire- Franz Ferdinand

ABOUT THE AUTHOR

Alexander Greengaard, MFA is an Instructor/Lecturer in the IBEST Program at Pima Community College. He works with students who have faced barriers to education and fights to break those barriers through integrated education and training initiatives, partnerships between basic education and college trade certification programs, and developing open educational materials. Alexander is also the founder of Troubadour, an arts education organization that provides theatre programs to economically marginalized families. Upcoming releases, press, and author updates can be found at hialex.net.